NEW YORK REVIEW BOOKS
CLASSICS

RED LIGHTS

GEORGES SIMENON (1903–1989) was born in Liège, Belgium. He went to work as a reporter at the age of fifteen and in 1923 moved to Paris, where under various pseudonyms he became a highly successful and prolific author of pulp fiction while leading a dazzling social life. In the early 1930s, Simenon emerged as a writer under his own name, gaining renown for his detective stories featuring Inspector Maigret. He also began to write his psychological novels, or *romans durs*—books in which he displays a sympathetic awareness of the emotional and spiritual pain underlying the routines of daily life. Having written nearly two hundred books under his own name and become the best-selling author in the world, Simenon retired as a novelist in 1973, devoting himself instead to dictating memoirs that filled thousands of pages.

ANITA BROOKNER is an art historian and novelist. She lives in London.

RED LIGHTS

GEORGES SIMENON

Translated from the French by

NORMAN DENNY

Introduction by

ANITA BROOKNER

NEW YORK REVIEW BOOKS

New York

THIS IS A NEW YORK REVIEW BOOK
PUBLISHED BY THE NEW YORK REVIEW OF BOOKS
435 Hudson Street, New York, NY 10014
www.nyrb.com

First published in French as *Feux Rouges*, 1953
First published in the United States, 1955

Library of Congress Cataloging-in-Publication Data
Simenon, Georges, 1903–1989.
[Feux rouges. English]
Red lights / by Georges Simenon ; translated by Norman Denny ; introduction by Anita Brookner.
p. cm. — (New York Review Books classics)
ISBN-13: 978-1-59017-193-6 (alk. paper)
ISBN-10: 1-59017-193-4 (alk. paper)
I. Denny, Norman, 1901– II. Title. III. Series.
PQ2637.I53F4813 2006
843'.912—dc22
2006014821

ISBN 978-1-59017-193-6

Printed in the United States of America on acid-free paper.
10 9 8 7 6 5 4 3

INTRODUCTION

FATE WAS kind to Georges Simenon: it gave him fame and wealth in his lifetime. Today he is perhaps little more than a familiar name, creator of Inspector Maigret, the second-most-famous detective in the annals of crime fiction, Sherlock Holmes being the first. But he is remembered with particular veneration by those who experienced the excitement of his almost industrial output of novels in the Paris of the 1950s, a place and a time still bearing vestigial traces of hardship and humiliation, and just beginning to retrieve a sense of national self-reliance. To that sense Simenon was a major contributor, no less a figure in his day than Gide and Bernanos, before Sartre and Camus imprinted their identity and their more lasting fame on a reading public primed to take up the challenge of a morality which has become commonplace, but one to which Simenon was no stranger.

In his heyday he was read largely but not exclusively by the people for whom he preferred to write, the *petites gens* of his own early milieu, who would understand and appreciate not only his pared-down style but also his intimate fatalism, before such a condition was codified by more sophisticated writers as alienation. The unease which underlies this condition is already present in Simenon's novels, and is most potently expressed not in the detective stories featuring Inspector Maigret but in the *romans durs*, the hard novels of which he was more proud.

The formula is simple but subtle. A life will go wrong, usually because of an element in the protagonist's make-up which impels him to self-destruct, to willfully seek disgrace, exclusion, ruin in his search for a fulfillment and a fatal freedom which take on an aura of destiny.

In a genre which has since been exploited, but never truly replicated, Simenon examines this phenomenon time after time and in a variety of settings. A man (and it is almost invariably a man) will suddenly act out of character and for no apparent reason. This divergence from his normal pattern of behavior will lead him to abandon all safety, all caution, in the interest of that illusory freedom. This momentary rapture, against which he has no defense, will ensure his downfall, but the rash act will empower him in ways he has perhaps sought, almost unknowingly, all his life.

This dilemma is set out in a manner and a style which ensure immediate understanding. Simenon deliberately scaled down his vocabulary to ensure that no potential reader, however humble, was excluded. He is thus a truly democratic writer, almost an artisan, a man who believed in an honest day's work. Yet there was nothing simple or typical about his working life. He reckoned to complete a novel in five, or six, or at most eleven days, and to this end would labor in an almost fetishistic trance: his sweat-soaked lumberjack's shirt would be laundered every night, ready for him to wear the following morning, and so on until the brief spasm was over. Then relief would be sought in equally compulsive sexual activity, the two methods being almost interchangeable.

After undistinguished beginnings in journalism and pulp fiction, Simenon graduated to a position which many writers would envy: a large household, a vast disposable income, and the greatest freedom of all, the freedom to give it all up, which he did, abruptly, and equally without warning, some years before his death in 1989, after a career spanning forty years, in the course of which he produced some two hundred novels, few of which are as simple as they appear or were intended to be.

Just such a novel is *Red Lights*, originally published as *Feux Rouges* in 1955, perhaps the optimum year for Simenon's fiction. It is untypical only in the sense that the action takes place in America; apart from that all the familiar elements are in place. The story begins quietly enough. Steve and Nancy Hogan are driving to pick up their children from camp in Maine. It is Labor Day and traffic is thick on the roads. Steve feels in need of a drink, or several drinks, which irritates his wife; she decides to leave him the car and to travel on by bus. He in his turn is irritated, and after a few drinks "goes into the tunnel," a kind of mental fugue. This is a secret process which he invariably regrets. But he is on his own, and free, free to talk to strangers and to explain to them at some length the differences between men and women, and what it feels like to be a man. By now he has stopped several times and has gone so far off the road that there is no point in trying to find the correct exit. In one of the bars he visits he hears on the radio that a prisoner has escaped from Sing Sing and has locked a child in a cupboard. He pays little attention to this, but when he finds a stranger in his car he knows immediately who he is. He accepts the situation almost without thought, almost glad of the company, and continues his monologue, to which the convict, not unnaturally, makes no reply.

From then on matters deteriorate. Steve passes out. When he comes to, after several hours of drunken sleep, the convict has gone, and so has his wallet. On the grass verge on which he is lying, his wife's clothes, taken from their suitcase, are scattered around, and the car has a flat tire. He rings the children's camp, and learns that Nancy has never arrived. A friendly waitress in a diner tells him that a woman was attacked on the highway the previous night and taken to the hospital. After many telephone calls he locates the hospital and finds his wife, who shrinks from him in terror. The police have become involved. There is a sort of resolution, but nothing will ever be the same again, simply because Steve obeyed an inconvenient desire to abandon his wife and go in search of a drink. The novel is a masterly demonstration of an impulse all the more natural for being entirely instinctive, almost defiant. In obeying this impulse Steve has gone "into the tunnel."

The ease and speed of the narrative, together with the faultless detail, might incline one to think of this as a typical American thriller of its time. Only the painful presence of Steve's unconscious prompting betrays Simenon's interest in, and understanding of, altered states. Going into the tunnel, as experienced by Steve, and undoubtedly by Simenon himself, signifies a compulsion to throw off the constraints imposed by conformity, and a surrender to the forces of the mind which remain mysterious even when—particularly when—they have been acted upon. For Simenon going into the tunnel meant writing novel after novel: that perhaps is not in itself mysterious. What remains singular is his ability to turn this compulsion into stories which are entirely lucid, which deal with commonplace events, and which betray only a fraction of the dread experienced by both the characters and their author. Thus each novel is obliged to dwell on the same theme. The peculiar talent, even genius, of Simenon is to write stories which, although they contain and indeed explicate this dread, remain accessible to all.

—Anita Brookner

RED LIGHTS

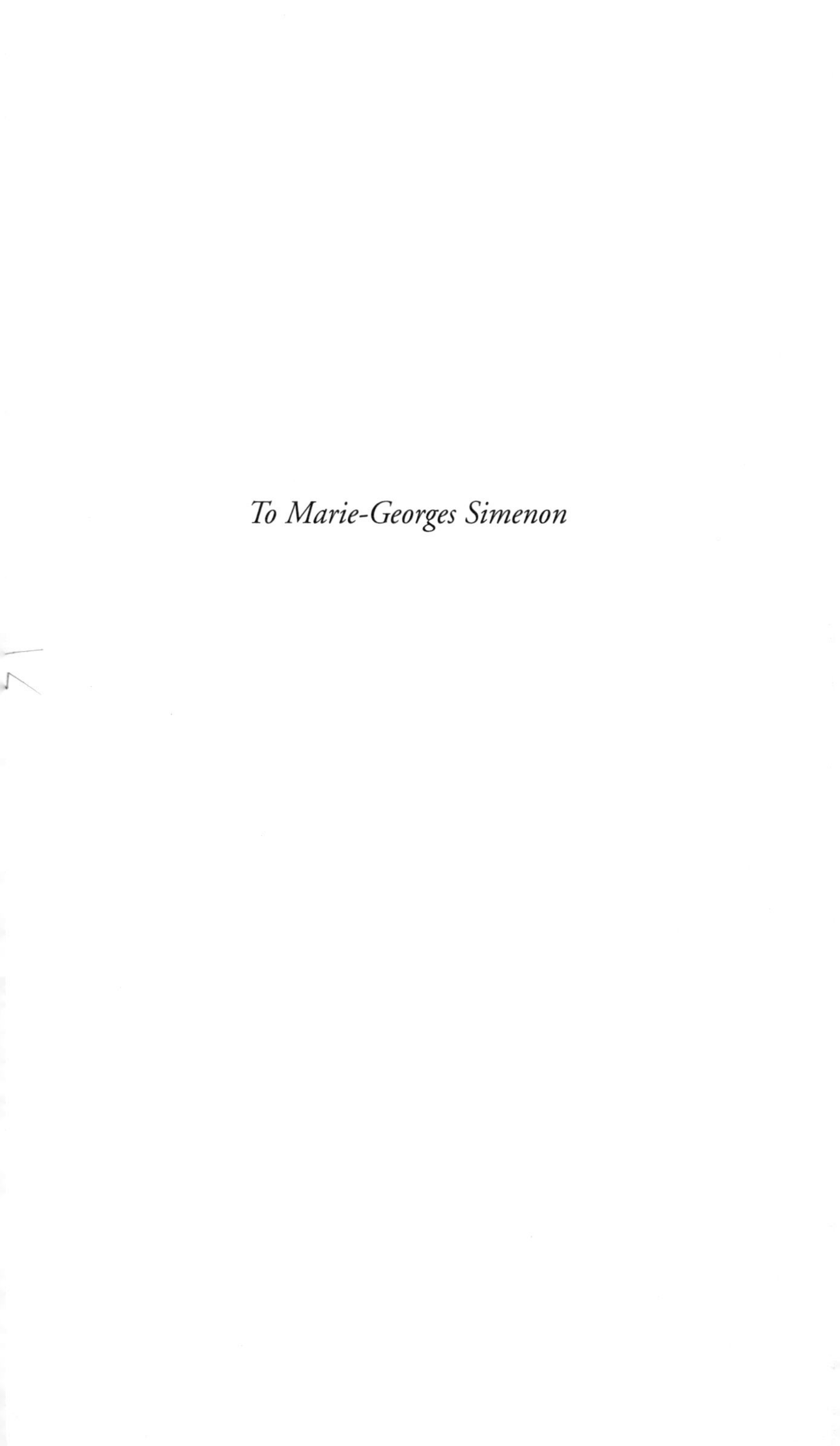

To Marie-Georges Simenon

1

HE CALLED it "going into the tunnel," an expression of his own, for his private use, which he never used in talking to anyone else, least of all to his wife. He knew exactly what it meant, and what it was like to be in the tunnel; yet, curiously, when he was there he never allowed himself to admit the fact, except for occasional brief instants, and always too late. As for determining the precise moment when he entered it, he had often tried to do this afterwards, but never with success.

Today, for example, he had started Labor Day weekend in the best of spirits. The same thing had happened on other occasions. It had also happened that the weekend nevertheless finished badly. But there was no reason why this should be inevitable.

He left his office on Madison Avenue at five o'clock, and three minutes later had joined his wife at their little bar on Forty-fifth Street, where she had arrived first and had ordered a martini without waiting for him. There were not many regular customers in the dimly lighted room. In fact, he did not see a single face he knew, because everyone was rushing, even more hurriedly than on other Fridays, for the cars and trains that would take them to the sea or into the country. Within an hour New York would be deserted except, in the quiet districts, for men in their shirt sleeves and bare-legged women seated in their doorways.

It was not yet raining. Since first thing that morning, and indeed for the past three days, the sky had been overcast, the air so laden with moisture that one could gaze steadily at the yellow splash of the sun as though looking at it through a pane of frosted glass. The weather forecasts were now predicting local storms and holding out hopes of a cooler night.

"Tired?"

"Not very."

They met there at the same time every evening in the summer, when the children were away at camp, always sitting on the same stools, and Louis, the barman, would greet them with a wink and start mixing their drinks without waiting for the order. They felt no need to start talking at once. One would offer the other a cigarette. Sometimes Nancy would push the dish of peanuts toward him, or he would pass her the olives, while they gazed absently at the small, pallid rectangle of the television receiver set high in the right-hand corner of the bar. Images flickered across it. A voice poured out a commentary on a baseball game, or a woman sang. It was quite unimportant.

"You'll be able to take a shower before we start."

It was her way of looking after him. She never failed to ask if he was tired, darting at him the sort of look one gives a delicate child or one that seems to be sickening for something. It ruffled him slightly. He knew he did not look his best at that time, with his shirt sticking to his body and his beard beginning to show, seeming darker against the skin softened by the heat. She was bound to have noticed the damp circles under his armpits.

It was the more irritating since she herself was as fresh as she had been when she left the house that morning, without a crease in her lightly starched linen suit, so that no one would have supposed, from the look of her, that she had spent the day in an office. She might have been taken for one of those women who don't get up before four in the afternoon, and make their first appearance at cocktail time.

Louis asked:

"You going to get the kids?"

Steve nodded.

"New Hampshire?"

"Maine."

How many parents were there, in New York and the suburbs, who that evening would be setting off along the roads to bring their children home from the camps up North? A hundred thousand? Two hundred thousand? Probably more. The figure must be tucked away in some corner of the newspaper. And then there were the children who had spent the summer with an aunt or grandmother in the country or by the sea. And it was the same everywhere, from one seaboard to the other, from the Canadian frontier right down to Mexico.

From the television screen a man in shirt sleeves, wearing thickly rimmed glasses that seemed to make him feel hot, announced in a tone of gloomy conviction:

"The National Safety Council predicts that this evening between forty and forty-five million motorists will be on the roads, and it estimates that between now and Monday evening four hundred and thirty-five people will have lost their lives in road accidents."

He finished lugubriously, before making way for a beer advertisement:

"Don't be one of them. Drive carefully."

Why four hundred and thirty-five, and not four hundred and thirty or four hundred and forty? Sandwiched between the regular programs, the prediction would be repeated all that night, and tomorrow and the next day, until toward the end they acquired the suspense of a race commentary. Steve recalled the voice of a speaker last year, when they were bringing the children back from Maine on the Sunday evening:

"Up to now the number of deaths is considerably lower than the official forecast, despite the collision of two air liners over Washington Airport, in which thirty-two people lost their lives. But watch out! The weekend isn't over yet!"

"Myself," said Louis, talking as usual in an undertone and bringing a fresh supply of peanuts, "my wife and kid are with my mother-in-law, near Quebec. They're coming back by train tomorrow."

Had Steve meant to order another martini? As a rule Nancy and he had only one, except occasionally when they dined in town before going to the theater.

Perhaps he had wanted to; not necessarily to give himself a lift or because of the heat. In fact, for no special reason. Or rather, because this was not an ordinary weekend. When they got back from Maine there would be no more thought of summer or of vacations; it would be winter setting in, the days growing shorter, and the children at home, obliging them to come straight back from the office; a more complicated life altogether, without any letup.

Didn't that rate another drink? He had not said anything, had made no movement, no sign to Louis. But Nancy guessed what was in his mind, and at once slipped down from her stool.

"You'd better pay. It's time we were going."

He wasn't really angry about it. A bit disappointed perhaps, slightly put out. What did irritate him was that Louis had known perfectly well what was going on.

They had to cross two streets to reach the car park where they left their car for the day, and, once past Third Avenue, one might have thought it was a Sunday.

"Do you want me to drive?" said Nancy.

He said no, took his place at the wheel, drove toward the Queensboro Bridge, where the procession of cars was moving at a snail's pace. Two hundred yards farther on a car had already been turned over at the edge of the sidewalk, and a woman was seated on the ground with people crowding round her and a policeman trying to keep traffic moving along until the arrival of an ambulance.

"There's no point in leaving too soon," said Nancy, feeling

in her handbag for cigarettes. "In an hour or two the worst of the crush will be over."

A few drops rolled down the windshield as they drove through Brooklyn, but the rain that had been forecast had not yet really started.

He was in a good mood at that moment, and still was when they reached their home in Scottville, a new development in the middle of Long Island.

"Do you mind if we just have something cold?"

"I'd prefer it."

The house, too, would be different once the children were back. During the summer he always had a feeling of aimlessness, as though the two of them had no reason for being there, or for being in one room more than another, and they were constantly at a loss to know what to do with their evenings.

"While you're making sandwiches I'll run out and get some cigarettes."

"There are some in the cupboard."

"Well, it'll save time if I fill up with gas and oil."

She made no objection to this, which surprised him. And he did in fact go to the garage. While they were checking the tires he darted into the Italian restaurant to have a whiskey at the bar.

"Scotch?"

"Rye."

Yet he didn't really like rye. He had chosen the stronger of the two because he would probably not have another chance for a drink that night, and they'd be driving for hours along the highway.

Could one say that he had entered the tunnel? He had had only two drinks, no more than when they went to the theater and Nancy drank the same as he did....

"Did you get cigarettes?"

"You said there were some in the cupboard. I filled up with gas and had the tires checked."

"We'll get some as we go."

There weren't any cigarettes in the house. Either she had made a mistake or she had deliberately told him otherwise.

She stopped him as he was on his way to the bathroom.

"You can have your shower after we've eaten, while I'm stacking the dishes."

She didn't order him about, actually, but she arranged their life in her own way, as though it were the natural thing to do. He was wrong. He knew he was wrong. Whenever he had had a drink or two he saw her differently, becoming annoyed by things that ordinarily he took for granted.

"You'd better take your tweed jacket and your raincoat."

A breeze was rising outside, stirring the leaves of the still-slender trees that had been planted five years before, when the houses had been built and the streets laid out. Some had never taken root, and two or three attempts to replace them had been failures.

Across the way one of their neighbors was attaching a trailer with a canoe on it to his car, while his wife, flushed with recent sunburn, her fat thighs filling pale blue shorts, stood at the edge of the sidewalk holding the fishing rods.

"What are you thinking about?"

"Nothing special."

"I wonder if Dan's grown any more. Last month I thought he was taller, and his legs looked thinner."

"It's normal at his age."

Nothing particular happened. He had his shower, got dressed, and then his wife reminded him to go and pull the main electricity switch in the garage while she went around to see that all the windows were closed.

"Shall I take the bags?"

"Make sure they're shut tight."

Despite the breeze and the lowering sky, his clean shirt was damp by the time he got in behind the wheel.

"Shall we go the same way as last time?"

"We swore we'd never go that way again."

"Just the same, it's the best."

Less than a quarter of an hour later they were wedged in among thousands of other cars moving in the same direction, with inexplicable holdups and occasional, momentary bursts of almost frantic speed.

It was at the beginning of Merritt Parkway that they ran into their first thunderstorm, when darkness had not quite fallen and the cars had switched on only their parking lights. There were three lanes of traffic between the white lines heading north, but many fewer, of course, coming the opposite way, and one could hear the rain drumming on the steel roofs, the monotonous swish of the wheels throwing up a spray of water, the irritating sweep-sweep of the windshield wiper.

"Sure you aren't tired?"

"Certain."

Sometimes one file got ahead of the others and sometimes one had a sense of losing ground.

"You should have gotten into the third lane."

"I'm trying."

"Not now. There's a fool behind us."

At every lightning flash one had a glimpse of faces in the darkened interiors of the adjacent cars, all with the same strained expression.

"Cigarette?"

"Thanks, I'd like one."

She always passed them to him lighted when he was driving.

"Like the radio on?"

"I don't mind."

But she had to switch it off again because of the static caused by the storm.

It was not worth the effort of talking, either. The constant hubbub made it necessary to raise one's voice, which soon became tiring. Gazing straight ahead, he had a sidelong vision of Nancy's profile, palely shining in the half-light, and he asked her several times:

"What are you thinking about?"

"Nothing special."

Once she added:

"And you?"

He said:

"About the children."

It was not true. In fact he was not thinking about anything special either. To be precise, he was sorry he had managed to slide into the third traffic lane, because it would be difficult to change without his wife asking why. Yet in a little while, when they had left the parkway, there would be bars along the side of the road.

Had they ever driven the children to or from camp without his pulling in a few times for a drink? Only once, three years ago, when he had had a terrible scene with Nancy the night before, and, both deeply shaken, they had made the weekend into a second honeymoon.

"We seem to have left the storm behind."

She turned off the windshield wiper, but had to turn it on again for a few minutes because big, isolated drops continued to splash against the glass.

"You're not cold?"

"No."

The air had grown cool. With one elbow thrust out of the window, Steve could feel the wind blowing under his shirt sleeve.

"And you?"

"Not yet. I'll put on my coat in a little while."

Why did they feel an obscure need to exchange remarks of this sort? Was it to reassure themselves? If so, what were they afraid of?

"Now that the storm's over I'll try the radio again."

There was music. Nancy gave him another cigarette, and, lighting one herself, lay back in her seat, blowing the smoke above her head.

"Special report of the Connecticut Automobile Club..."

So they were already in Connecticut, fifty miles from New London.

"Labor Day weekend claimed its first victim in Connecticut at 7:45 this evening, when at the intersection of Highways 1 and 118, at Darien, a private car driven by Mr. MacKillian, of New York, collided with a truck driven by Robert Ostling. MacKillian and his passenger, John Roe, were killed instantly. The truck driver was uninjured. Ten minutes later, thirty miles from there, a car driven by..."

He switched it off. His wife opened her mouth to say something and then stopped. Had she noticed that, perhaps unconsciously, he had slowed down a little?

She finally said:

"Past Providence there'll be less traffic."

"Yes—until we run into the Boston mob."

He was not shaken by the accident reports, not alarmed. What got on his nerves was the incessant hum of wheels on either side of him, the headlights rushing to meet him every hundred yards, and also the sensation of being caught in a tide, with no way of escaping either to right or to left, or even of driving more slowly, because his mirror showed a triple string of lights following bumper-to-bumper behind him.

Neon signs had begun to flash by on the right, where, with the gasoline pumps, they were the only manifestation of life. Except for them one might have thought that the highway was suspended in space, and that nothing existed beyond it but night and silence. The towns, the villages were set farther back, and only rarely did a vague, reddish glow in the sky give a hint of their existence.

The only immediate reality was that of the restaurants and bars that sprang out of the darkness every few miles, their signs advertising in red, green, and blue letters brands of beer or whiskey.

He was now in the second traffic lane. He had edged gradually into it without his wife's noticing, and suddenly, seeing a gap, he slid into the first.

"What are you doing?"

He nearly overshot a bar whose neon sign announced, "The Little Cottage," braked just in time, so abruptly that the car behind had to make a sudden swerve and a flood of abuse poured from it. The driver even shook his fist out of the window.

"I have to go to the men's room," he said, keeping his voice as natural as possible while he pulled up at the side of the road. "You aren't thirsty?"

"No."

It often happened. She would wait for him in the car. In another car parked in front of the bar a couple embraced so closely that for a moment he wondered whether they were one person or two.

A moment later, pushing open the door, he felt a different man, and he paused for an instant to survey the room bathed in a dim orange light. This bar was like all the others along the road, and not so very different from Louis's place on Forty-fifth Street, with the same television set in the corner, the same smells, the same lights.

"Dry martini with a lemon peel," he said as the barman turned to him.

"Single?"

"Double."

If he hadn't been asked, he would have settled for a single, but a double was better, because his wife probably wouldn't allow him to stop again.

He hesitated, glancing toward the door of the toilet, and

then dutifully started for it from a sort of honesty, passing a man with very dark hair who was telephoning with a hand curved round the side of his mouth. His voice was harsh.

"Yes. Just tell him what I told you. Nothing else. He'll understand. I tell you, he'll understand, see?"

Steve would have liked to hear more, but the man glanced at him as he spoke with a far from encouraging look. What was it all about? Who was at the other end of the line?

He came back to the bar and emptied his glass in two gulps, feeling in his pocket for the money. Would Nancy hold her tongue? Wasn't it bad enough that just because of her he couldn't stay there a few minutes, simply to look at people and relax his nerves?

Perhaps he had now entered the tunnel. Perhaps he had been in it ever since they left Long Island. If so, he was not aware of the fact, and thought himself the most normal man on earth, not in the least affected by the one or two drinks he had had.

Why did he feel uncomfortable, even guilty, as he went toward the car and got in without looking at his wife? She asked no questions, made no comment.

"That's better!" he murmured as though to himself, starting the engine.

It seemed to him now that there were fewer cars on the road, that the pace had slackened, so much so that he passed three or four that were really going too slowly. An ambulance coming the other way left him unmoved, his attention being occupied at that moment by strange lights, then by a white barrier which suddenly loomed in front of them.

"Detour," said Nancy's calm voice, a little too expressionless.

"I can see."

"On the left."

This made him blush, because he had nearly turned right.

He grumbled:

"We've never once come this way without having to turn off somewhere! Why can't they repair the road in winter!"

"In the snow?" she asked in the same voice.

"Well, in the fall—anyway, some time when there aren't forty million motorists on the roads."

"You've passed the intersection."

"What intersection?"

"The one marked with an arrow showing the way back to the highway."

"What about the people behind us?" he asked sarcastically.

There were still cars following—fewer than there had been, however.

"Everybody isn't going to Maine."

"Don't you worry. I'll get you to Maine all right."

A moment later he seemed to have triumphed, because they were emerging on to a major road.

"Well? What about your arrow now?"

"This isn't Highway 1."

"We'll soon know."

What set his nerves on edge was her self-confidence, the calmness with which she answered him.

He persisted:

"I suppose you can't be wrong, can you?"

She said nothing, and this irritated him still more.

"Go on! Say what you want to say!"

"Do you remember the time when we made a detour of sixty miles?"

"And dodged the worst of the traffic!"

"But without meaning to!"

"Listen, Nancy, if you want to start a quarrel why not say so?"

"I'm not trying to quarrel. I'm trying to find out where we are."

"Well, as I'm driving, do me a favor and don't fuss!"

She remained silent. He did not recognize the road either. It was narrower and not so good, without a single filling station since they had entered it; and another storm was rumbling in the sky.

Nancy quietly took the road map out of the glove compartment and switched on the light on the dashboard.

"We must be between 1 and 82, on a road going to Norwich, but I can't find the number."

She tried, too late, to catch the name of a village that sprang up out of the darkness; and then they had left its few lights behind and were passing through woods.

"Don't you really think we should turn back?"

"No."

With the map still on her knees she lit a cigarette, without offering him one.

"Furious?" he said.

"Me?"

"Yes, you! Why not admit you're furious? Just because I happened to miss the highway and we have to go a few extra miles! I seem to remember that not long ago you were saying we had any amount of time."

"Watch out!"

"What for?"

"You nearly went off the road."

"So now I don't know how to drive?"

"I didn't say that."

And then the words burst from him, for no precise reason.

"No, you didn't say it, but now I'm going to say something, my pet, and you might as well get it into your head, once and for all..."

The strangest thing was that he had no idea what he was going to say. He groped round for something strong, decisive; something to give his wife a good dose of the humility she so badly needed.

"You see, Nancy, maybe you're the only person who doesn't know it, but you're a pest."

"Watch the road, will you!"

"Sure I'll watch the road! And I'll drive nice and carefully, so as not to go off the tracks. Do you know what tracks I'm talking about?"

It seemed to him extremely subtle, and dazzling in its truth. Almost as though he had made a new discovery. What was wrong with Nancy, finally, was that she always stayed on the tracks, never allowed herself the least diversion.

"You don't understand, do you?"

"Do I have to?"

"What? Do you have to know what I think? God almighty, it might at least help you to try and understand other people and make life a bit more pleasant for them. For me, in particular. Only I doubt if you care."

"Wouldn't you let me drive?"

"No, I wouldn't. Just for the sake of argument, suppose instead of always thinking of yourself and being so damned sure you're right, you took a good look at yourself in the mirror and asked yourself..."

He was laboriously struggling to express something he felt, which he was convinced he had felt every day of his life throughout the eleven years they had been married. It was not the first time it had happened, but now he was sure he had made a discovery that would enable him to explain everything. She would have to understand sometime, wouldn't she? And the day she understood, maybe she'd try and treat him like a grown man.

"Can you think of anything more senseless than to be like a train, always following the same route along the same tracks? Well, just now on the parkway I had the feeling I was like a train. Other cars were pulling up and men were getting out without having to ask anyone's leave to go and have a glass of beer. And..."

"Did you have a beer?"

He hesitated, decided upon frankness.

"No."

"A martini?"

"Yes."

"A double?"

It infuriated him to have to answer:

"Yes."

"And before that?" she was unkind enough to insist.

"Before what?"

"Before we left."

"I don't understand."

"What did you drink when you went to fill up with gas?" This time he lied.

"Nothing."

"Oh?"

"You don't believe me?"

"If it's true, a double martini hit you harder than usual."

"You think I'm drunk?"

"You're certainly talking the way you do when you've been drinking."

"Meaning, I'm not making sense?"

"I don't know if it's sense or not, but I know you hate me."

"Why don't you try to understand?"

"Understand what?"

"That I don't hate you, that I love you, in fact that I'd be perfectly happy with you if you'd treat me as a grown man."

"By letting you drink at every bar along the way?"

"You see!"

"What am I supposed to see?"

"You have to put it in the most humiliating way you can. You deliberately exaggerate everything. Am I a drunk?"

"Of course not. I'd never have married a drunk."

"Do I often have too much?"

"Not very."

"Not even once a month. Perhaps once in three months."

"Well, then, what's the matter with you?"

"There wouldn't be anything the matter with me if you didn't treat me like a worm. Just because for one evening I'd like to get a little outside everyday life!"

"Does it cramp you so much?"

"I didn't say that. Take Dick, for instance. I don't suppose he ever goes to bed less than half tight. But that doesn't stop you thinking how interesting he is, and you talk seriously to him by the hour, even when he's been drinking."

"For one thing, he isn't my husband."

"And what else?"

"There's a truck ahead of us."

"I can see."

"Be quiet a minute. We're coming to a crossroad and I want to see what's on the road sign."

"You don't like me talking about Dick?"

"I don't mind."

"You're sorry you didn't marry him instead of me?"

"No."

They were on the highway again, with two lines of cars traveling very much faster than in the outskirts of New York, and overtaking furiously. Perhaps in the hope of silencing him, Nancy switched on the radio, which was giving out the eleven-o'clock news.

"... The police have reason to believe that Sid Halligan, who escaped last night from Sing Sing Penitentiary, and has so far evaded his pursuers..."

She turned it off again.

"Why did you switch off?"

"I didn't think you were interested."

He wasn't interested. He had never heard of Sid Halligan, did not even know that a prisoner had escaped from Sing Sing the night before. He had merely thought, as he heard the words, of the man telephoning in the bar, with his hand cupped round his mouth and a fierce glare in his eyes. There was nothing to it, except for her switching off the radio without asking him, but it is trifles such as these . . .

Where had they got to when she had broken off the argument? They had been talking about Dick Lowell, who had married a friend of Nancy, and with whom they sometimes spent an evening.

Hell, what was the good of arguing? Did Dick care what his wife thought . . . ? The mistake he made was that he was always worrying about what Nancy thought, and always trying to win her approval.

"What are you doing?"

"Stopping, that's what."

"Listen . . . !"

This bar had a shabby look, with nothing but a few half-broken-down cars outside, and that made him all the more anxious to go in.

"If you stop," Nancy was saying, carefully pronouncing each syllable, "I warn you I'll go on alone."

It gave him a shock. For an instant he stared at her, incredulous, and she met his gaze steadily. She was as trim and neat as when they had left New York—cool as a cucumber, he thought.

Perhaps nothing would have happened, and he would have given way, if she had not added:

"You can always come on to the camp by bus."

He felt his lip twist in a queer sort of smile and, as calm as she was herself, he reached for the ignition key, which he took out and put in his pocket.

Nothing of the kind had ever happened to them before. He could not turn back now. He was convinced that she needed a lesson.

He got out of the car and shut the door without looking at

her, and made himself walk with a steady stride toward the entrance of the bar. When he looked around from the doorway she had not moved, and he could see her pale profile through the glass.

He went in. Faces turned toward him, transformed by the smoke as though in the trick mirrors at a fair, and when he put his hand on the counter he felt it sticky with alcohol.

2

DURING the time it had taken him to cross from the door to the bar the conversation ceased, the hubbub of voices that had filled the room an instant before stopped with the abruptness of an orchestral ending. Everyone stayed motionless, their eyes following him without hostility, without interest, it seemed, and without its being possible to discern an expression on their faces.

After he had laid his hand on the counter, and the barman had reached out a hairy arm to wipe it with a dirty cloth, life had been resumed and no one seemed to pay him any further attention.

He had been struck by this. The bar was very different from the usual roadside places. There must be a village quite near, or a small town, probably a factory, because the people were talking with different accents and two Negroes were leaning against the bar near him.

"What'll it be, stranger?" asked the man behind the counter.

He had not used the word facetiously. His voice was friendly.

"Rye," murmured Steve.

He ordered it this time, not because it was stronger, but because here he would have attracted notice by ordering scotch. He did not want to leave Nancy alone too long. On the other hand, he must not return to the car too soon, or his gesture would be wasted.

He was dismayed by the firm line he had taken. And half inclined to be ashamed, although in his heart he was convinced that he was within his rights and that his wife deserved a lesson.

Thanks to her, he scarcely knew places like this, and he breathed in the heavy atmosphere with relish, contemplating the dark green painted walls adorned with old lithographs and gazing through an open doorway into an untidy kitchen where a woman with gray hair falling over her face was drinking with two other women and a man.

A very large, old-type television screen was fixed above the bar. The quivering, streaked pictures splintered in a way that reminded one of very old films, and no one bothered to look at them; nearly everyone was talking loudly; one of the Negroes standing next to him kept jostling him as he stepped back to gesticulate, and each time apologized with a loud laugh. At a corner table two middle-aged lovers sat with their arms round each other's waist, cheeks pressed together, motionless as in a photograph, silent, their gaze lost in space.

Nancy would never understand all this. Even he would have found it difficult to explain to her what there was to understand. She thought he had stopped simply for the sake of having a drink, and it wasn't true; it was precisely her kind of truth that made her seem to be invariably in the right.

He was not angry with her. He wondered if she were crying, out there alone in the car, and he got a dollar bill out of his pocket and laid it on the counter. It was time to be going. He had been there about five minutes. A photograph suddenly appeared on the television screen, the picture of a little girl about four years old, huddled in a closet with brooms and buckets; he did not listen to the commentary, and the picture was replaced by one of a shop front with a smashed windowpane.

He was picking up his change, just about to turn away, when he felt a hand on his shoulder and heard a voice say, pronouncing the words with care:

"Have one on me, brother!"

It was the man on his right, whom he had scarcely noticed. He was by himself, leaning on the counter, and when Steve looked at him he stared back with an uncomfortable fixity. He must have had a lot to drink. His voice was thick, his movements studied, as though he knew his balance was uncertain.

Steve was inclined to refuse, saying that his wife was waiting for him. The man, guessing what was in his mind, turned to the barman and pointed to their empty glasses, and the barman gave Steve a slight nod, which meant "You can take it."

Or perhaps he was really saying, "You'd better accept it."

The man wasn't a noisy drunk. Indeed, was he a habitual drunkard at all? His white shirt was as clean as Steve's, his fair hair newly cut, and his sun-tanned skin brought out the pale blue of his eyes.

With his eyes fixed upon Steve he raised his glass, and Steve raised his own and emptied it at a gulp.

"Thanks. My wife..."

He broke off, because of the smile that spread over the other's face. It was as though this man who continued to stare steadily at him and said nothing knew everything, knew him like a brother, read his thoughts in his eyes.

He was drunk certainly, but in his drunkenness there was the bitter and smiling serenity of a being who has achieved Lord knows what superior wisdom.

Steve was in a hurry to get back to Nancy, and at the same time he feared to disappoint this man he did not know, who must be about his own age.

Turning to the barman, he said:

"The same."

He would have liked to talk, but could think of nothing to say. Silence, however, did not trouble the man and he continued to gaze at Steve with satisfaction, as though they were friends of long standing who had no need to talk.

Only when he tried to light a cigarette with a shaking hand did the degree of his intoxication become apparent, and he realized it, and his look, and the twist of his lip, seemed to say:

"Sure I've had a lot to drink! I'm drunk. So what?"

That gaze expressed so many things that Steve felt as uncomfortable as if he had been undressed in public.

"I know. Your wife's waiting for you in the car. She's going to make a scene. So what?"

Had he also guessed that he had children at a holiday camp in Maine? And a fifteen-thousand-dollar house on Long Island, payable in twelve years?

There must be an affinity between them, things in common that Steve would have liked to find out. But the thought that Nancy had now been waiting over ten minutes, perhaps a quarter of an hour, put him in a sort of panic.

He paid his round, awkwardly held out his hand, which the other man clasped, gazing into his eyes with so much insistence that he seemed to be trying to convey to him some mysterious message.

The same silence as when he entered accompanied him on his way out, and he did not venture to look around, opened the door, found that it had started to rain again. He noticed that a good many of the parked vehicles were delivery trucks, picked his way to his car, then stopped dead when he saw that his wife was not there.

At first he looked around him, thinking she had got out to stretch her legs. The rain was no longer heavy, but a fine, gentle drizzle with a pleasant coolness.

"Nancy!" he called in a low voice.

But there was not a pedestrian in sight on either side of the road. He was about to go back into the bar, to explain what had happened, and perhaps telephone the police, when, as he leaned in through the car window, he saw a scrap of paper on the seat. Nancy had torn it out of her diary and written:

"I'm going on by bus. Have a good trip!"

For the second time he was tempted to go back into the bar, this time to get drunk with the unknown friend. What caused him to change his mind was the sight of a cluster of lights about five hundred yards farther on. It was a crossroad where the long-distance busses probably stopped, and his wife must have walked in that direction. Perhaps he could still manage to catch her.

He started the engine, and as he drove peered out at the sides of the road, which, so far as he could tell in the darkness, was bordered by fields or open country.

He did not see anyone, reached the crossroad, and pulled up in front of a cafeteria from outside of which one could see its gleaming white walls, its chrome-nickel counter, two or three customers busy eating.

He ran in and asked:

"Do the busses stop here?"

A dark-haired, peaceful-looking woman engaged in making hot dogs answered:

"If you want the one for Providence, you've missed it. It went by five minutes ago."

"You haven't seen a fairly young woman in a light-colored suit? Or rather, she should have been wearing a gabardine coat..."

He suddenly remembered that he hadn't seen the coat in the car.

"She didn't come in here."

Without stopping to think he dashed out again, still agitated, conscious that he must look like a lunatic. A road went off to the right, the main street of a village, with the lighted window of a furniture store displaying a bed covered in blue satin. He did not trouble to ask where he was or to look at the map, but jumped into the car, started off noisily, and drove straight along the wet road.

The busses seldom went more than fifty miles an hour, and his idea was to overtake the one she was in, follow it to the next stopping place, where he would ask her to get back into the car; and she could drive if she wanted to.

He had been in the wrong. She was in the wrong too, but she would not admit it, and so, as usual, it was he who would end by apologizing. He started the windshield wipers, trod hard on the accelerator, and since both windows were open the wind ruffled his hair and, almost icily, blew down his neck.

Perhaps he talked to himself during those minutes while he stared ahead searching for the rear lights of the bus. He overtook ten, fifteen cars, of which two at least swerved abruptly at his passing. The sight of the speedometer needle touching seventy caused him a certain feverish excitement, and he almost wished a speed cop would come after him; he made up a story about it, about having to catch his wife at all costs, about the children waiting for them in Maine. Surely, in the circumstances, one was justified in breaking the rules?

He came to another lighted crossing, surrounded by gasoline pumps, where the road forked. At first glance one fork looked as good as the other. He did not slow up to choose, and not until he had covered another fifteen miles did he realize that he had gone wrong again.

He could have sworn just now that he was in Rhode Island. How and when had he come to turn back? He could not understand it, but the fact remained that he had been traveling away from his destination and that the road signs announced the town of Putnam, Connecticut.

It was no longer any use trying to overtake the bus. From now on Steve's time was all his own. Too bad for Nancy if she was furious. Too bad for him, too. Too bad for both of them!

He thought of trying to find the bar he had come from, but it would have been almost impossible. There would be others farther on, as many as he wanted, where, now that he was, so to speak, a bachelor, he could stop without having to make excuses.

The thing he was sorry about was not having had a chance to talk to the man who had laid a hand on his shoulder and offered him a rye. He remained convinced that they would have understood one another. It wasn't just that they were the same age, but they were of the same build, the same light coloring, the same fair hair—like one another right down to their long, bony, square-tipped fingers.

He would have liked to know whether the man, too, had been brought up in a town, as he had, or whether he'd been born in the country.

He was more experienced than himself, he admitted. Very likely he wasn't married, or if he was, he didn't bother about his wife. Who knows? Steve wouldn't have been surprised to learn that he had children too, but had walked out on them and their mother.

Something of that sort must have happened to him. Anyway, he didn't worry about being at the office at nine o'clock sharp, and getting back in good time so that the baby-sitter could go home.

Because when Bonnie and Dan weren't in camp, that is to say, during the greater part of the year, it was not Nancy who got home early to look after them; it was he. Because in her office she was a person of importance, the right hand of Mr. Schwartz, head of the firm of Schwartz & Taylor, who came between ten and eleven in the morning and had a business lunch nearly every day, after which he worked till six or seven in the evening.

Had the man in the bar guessed? Did it show on his face? He wouldn't be surprised. After years of that sort of life it would be bound to show in one's expression.

And the car? It was registered in his name, granted, but his wife was the one who used it in the evening to drive back to

Scottville. And always with good reason! Because of her important position with Mr. Schwartz, so important that when, after the children were born, Steve had wanted her to stay at home, Mr. Schwartz had taken the trouble to come personally to persuade Nancy to go back to work.

On the stroke of five he, Steve, was free. He could make a dash for the Lexington Avenue subway station, get wedged in the crush, and at Brooklyn sprint for the bus that stopped at the end of their lot.

Altogether it didn't take more than three quarters of an hour, and he would find Ida, the colored girl who minded the children when they got back from school, with her hat on already. Her time must be valuable too. Everybody's time was valuable. Everybody's except his own...

"Hello, is that you? I'm going to be late again tonight. Don't expect me before seven, maybe half-past. Will you give the children their supper and put them to bed...?"

He was on Highway 6, less than ten miles from Providence, and he had had to slow down because he was caught in the stream of traffic again. What were they all thinking, the other men he could see seated at the wheels of cars? Most of them had women beside them. Some had children asleep on the back seat. He seemed to feel all around him the dismal weariness of waiting rooms and occasionally he heard a burst of music, or the officious voice of an announcer.

For some time now the wiper had been working unnecessarily, and on both sides of the road the restaurants and filling stations were becoming more numerous, drawing closer together to form an almost unbroken chain of lights, with a patch of darkness only every mile or so.

He longed for a glass of cold beer, but precisely because there was nothing to hold him back he was determined to choose the right place to stop. The last bar had left him with a sort of nostalgia and he would have liked to find another of the same kind; so he went past the places that looked too new, past the too showy signs.

A police car passed him with its siren going, then an ambulance, then another, and a little farther on he had to slow to a walking pace in a line of traffic that moved around two cars, one of which had literally climbed on top of the other.

He had time to see a man in a white shirt like himself, like his friend in the bar, with his hair disheveled and blood on his face, who was explaining something to the police with one arm gesturing toward a point in space.

How many dead had the experts predicted for the weekend? Four hundred and thirty-five. He remembered the exact figure. Therefore he wasn't drunk. The proof was that he had driven at seventy miles an hour without the least mishap.

Nancy, in the stifling half-darkness of the bus, with the other passengers sound asleep all around her, must be regretting her decision. She was fastidious about rubbing shoulders with the crowd. The smell of humanity prevailing in the bus must certainly be bothering her as much as the familiarities of her neighbors. She would have been thoroughly unhappy in that last bar. Was she something of a snob?

He preferred to go on a mile or two after the bottleneck created by the accident, and at the point where he eventually pulled onto the side of the road there were two places almost next door to one another, a pretentious establishment with a mauve neon sign, and then, beyond a gap which served as a parking lot, a one-story wooden building built like a log cabin.

This was the one he chose. Another proof that he wasn't drunk was that he remembered to take out the ignition key and to switch off the lights of the car.

At first glance this bar was less shabby than the other and the interior really was that of a log cabin, with wooden walls blackened by the years, big beams running across the ceiling, pewter and earthenware tankards on the shelves, and a panoply of rifles dating from the time of the Civil War.

The owner, short and plump in a white apron, his head bald, had retained a slight German accent. There was a beer pump, and the beer was served in huge glass steins.

He took a moment to find room for himself at the bar, nodded toward the beer pump without speaking, and then gazed around at the people in the room as though looking for someone.

And perhaps he really was looking for someone, without realizing it. There was no television set here, but a lighted jukebox, red and yellow, whose gleaming mechanism manipulated the records with a fascinating deliberation. In addition to the music that poured from it a small brown radio behind the bar was also playing, solely, it seemed, for the benefit of the proprietor, who bent down to listen to it whenever he had a moment to spare.

Steve drank his beer in big, thirsty gulps, wiped his mouth with the back of his hand, and said without an instant's pause:

"A rye!"

The beer had no taste. He wanted to recapture the oily flavor of Irish whiskey, which made him gasp a little whenever he drank it. He perched himself with one buttock on a stool, his elbows on the counter, in exactly the attitude of the stranger at the last bar.

His eyes were also blue, a slightly darker shade, and his shoulders certainly as broad, with the same swelling of the shirt sleeves over the biceps.

He drank more slowly now, listening with one ear to what the two men on his right were saying. They were drunk. Everybody in the place was more or less drunk and from time to time one heard a great burst of laughter or the smashing of a glass on the floor.

"...so I asked him what kind of a sucker he took me for—

twelve bucks a ton!—and when he saw I wasn't kidding he looked me right in the eyes, like this, and..."

Tons of what? Steve never found out. The conversation afforded no clue, and the man who was lecturing didn't seem to care, being more interested in trying to catch what was being said by the radio. Another news bulletin. The announcer was giving a list of accidents, one of which had been caused by a tree struck by lightning, which had fallen onto the roof of a car.

Then there was political news, but Steve did not listen, seized by a sudden desire to put a hand on the shoulder of his neighbor on the left, just as the stranger had done to him, and to say as nearly as possible in the same tone of voice, with the same impenetrable expression:

"Have one on me, brother."

Because the man on this side of him was also alone. But, unlike the other, he did not seem to be drunk, and the glass of beer in front of him was three quarters full.

He was a different type. Dark-haired, with a long face, sallow skin, dark eyes, and thin, extraordinarily flexible fingers, which he used from time to time to take the cigarette out of his mouth.

He had glanced at Steve as he entered, and had immediately looked away. Pulling a cigarette pack from his pocket, he found it empty and left the bar for a moment to go to the automatic machine.

This was when Steve noticed his boots. They were muddy and too large—big, farmer's boots that did not go with the rest of him. He was wearing no jacket or tie, simply a blue cotton shirt and dark trousers kept up by a wide belt.

Despite his cumbersome footgear he moved like a cat, contrived to come and go without touching anyone, returned to his stool with a cigarette between his lips, glanced quickly at Steve, who opened his mouth to speak to him.

He had to talk to someone. Since Nancy had wanted it this

way, this was his night, a chance that perhaps would never come again. So far as Nancy was concerned, all he had to do was to impress upon his mind, while it was still clear, that he must telephone the Keanes between five and six in the morning. By that time his wife would have reached the camp. As in the two previous years, the Keanes had kept a room for them in one of the bungalows, or at the very least a bed, because during Labor Day weekend it would have been hopeless to try and find anything elsewhere. It was the same everywhere, from one end to the other of the United States.

"Forty-five million motorists . . . !" he jeered in an undertone.

He had spoken deliberately to catch his neighbor's ear.

"Forty-five million men and women loose on the roads!"

This suddenly looked to him like a discovery and he thought seriously about it while he gazed at the dark-haired young man on his left.

"That's a thing you won't see in any other country on earth! Four hundred and thirty-five deaths by Monday night!"

At last he made the gesture he so longed to make, and tapped the man lightly on the shoulder.

"Have one on me?"

The other looked around at him without troubling to answer, but Steve let it go and called to the proprietor, bent over his tiny radio.

"Two!" he said, holding up two fingers.

"Two what?"

"Ask him what he wants."

The young man shook his head.

"Two ryes," said Steve obstinately.

He wasn't offended. He hadn't responded to the man in the other bar either.

"You married?" he asked.

The young man wore no wedding ring, but that didn't prove anything.

"Well, I've got a wife and two kids, a daughter of ten and a boy of eight. They're both in camp."

His neighbor was too young to have children that age. He wasn't more than twenty-three or -four. He probably wasn't even married.

"New York?"

He got an answer of sorts, since the other shook his head:

"You're from around these parts? Providence? Boston?"

A vague gesture that wasn't affirmative either.

"The funny thing is I don't really like rye. Do you like rye? I wonder if there's anybody who really likes rye!"

He emptied his glass and pointed to the one his companion had not touched.

"You don't want it? Well, O.K.—it's a free country. No offense. Another night maybe I wouldn't drink the stuff for a million dollars. Tonight it happens I'm on rye. That's the way it is. And if you want to know, it's my wife's fault."

At any other time he would have shied away from a man who talked as he was doing now. This he perceived in a momentary flash, and it mortified him.

But the next instant he had swung back to the conviction that this was the night of his life and that it was vitally important to explain this to his haggard-faced companion.

Perhaps the reason why he wasn't drinking was because he was sick? His face was gray, his lower lip had a sort of tic that now and then caused the cigarette to quiver. Steve even wondered if he took dope.

That would have disappointed him. Any kind of drug frightened him, marijuana, heroin, or anything else, and he always watched with mingled terror and embarrassment a customer at Louis's Bar, a pretty woman, still very young, who worked as a model and was said to be an addict.

"If you aren't married, maybe you've never asked yourself the question. And yet it's a vital question. People talk about all kinds of things that they think are important, but they're scared to talk about this. Take my wife. Am I right, or am I wrong . . . ?"

He had started badly and could not pick up the thread of his thought. In any case, that was not the root of the matter. It had to do with women, certainly, but indirectly. What he was trying to explain was something complicated, so subtle that he did not hope to get back to it.

At moments he seemed to have ten phrases on his lips at once, ten thoughts, each of which had its place in his chain of reasoning, but no sooner had he uttered a few words than he felt his task virtually impossible.

This depressed him.

"Same thing, boss!"

He nearly lost his temper when he saw the proprietor hesitate before serving him.

"Do I look like a drunk? Am I the kind of man to start a rumpus? I'm talking quietly to this boy here without even raising my voice . . . ."

The drink was served, and he gave a chuckle of satisfaction.

"That's better . . . What was I saying? I was talking about women, and about the highways. That's the whole point. Remember that. Women against highways, see? Women follow the tracks. Fine! They know where they're going. Even when they're still kids they know where they're heading for, and when you kiss them good night after a party they smell the orange blossom! Right . . . ?

"Mind you, I've got nothing against them! I'm just stating one of the facts of nature. . . ."

Women and railroad tracks . . . Men and highways . . . Because whatever they do, men have got something in here . . .

He thumped his chest with conviction, and in doing so again lost the thread of his argument. The words just wouldn't come.

"Men . . ." he repeated, making an effort.

He would have liked to explain what men need, what they

are deprived of through lack of understanding. That was where the difficulty lay. It wasn't a matter of drinking a certain number of ryes, as Nancy would have said sarcastically. The rye had nothing to do with it. What mattered on a night like this, for instance, a memorable night, when forty-five million motorists were loose on the roads, was to understand, and to understand it was necessary to go off the tracks.

Just as when he had gone into that other bar! Where else would he have met a man like the one he had got to know without any need to say anything? Certainly not at the office. His firm, World Travelers, also sold mileage: air mileage—trips in luxury aircrafts to London, Paris, Rome, or Cairo. To anywhere on earth. Every customer was in a hurry. It was indispensable, it was vitally important for each and every one to leave immediately.

Not at Schwartz & Taylor's, either, who sold publicity space —magazine pages, radio and television time, billboards along the roads.

Not even at Louis's Bar, where at five o'clock customers such as he came to the trough to restore themselves with a dry martini.

He suddenly wanted a martini, but he was sure the proprietor would not let him have it, and he did not want to risk a rebuff in the presence of his new friend.

"You see there are those that go off and those that don't, but that's that!"

He was still talking about the tracks. He was no longer precise. He even skipped unnecessary words, perhaps because they were difficult to pronounce.

"Take me. Tonight I've gone off..."

His earlier friend had very likely gone off the rails for good. So, too, perhaps, the man who, in the first bar, had been telephoning a mysterious message, a hand cupped around his mouth.

And what about this one? Steve was dying to ask; he kept winking at him to encourage him to talk about himself. He didn't work in an office, or on a farm, either: that was obvious, in spite of his heavy boots. Perhaps he was tramping along the roads, his pockets empty, hitchhiking when he could? Didn't he realize that it was nothing to be ashamed of? Far from it!

"Tomorrow I'll be with the kids. . . ."

At the thought he was overtaken by a wave of sentimentality that brought a lump to his throat, and it seemed to him suddenly that he was betraying Bonnie and Dan; he tried to picture them in his mind's eye, was unable to conjure up more than a hazy image, and got out his wallet to look at the snapshots he always carried with him.

He had not really meant to say that. He loved his children well enough and had no regrets for all he did for them; but the thing he was trying desperately to explain was that he was a man, and that . . .

He inserted his fingers under his driver's license to get out the snapshots, and his head was turned away when his companion laid a coin on the counter and started for the door. It was done so quickly, like the gliding away of a snake, that it was a moment before he realized what had happened.

"He's gone?" he asked, turning toward the proprietor.

"And good riddance!"

"You know him?"

"I don't want to know him."

He was rather shocked that the owner of a place such as this should be sticking to the rails too. Steve was the one who was drinking, not the young man—he hadn't even finished his beer—yet it was Steve who was being treated with a certain consideration, probably because his face showed that he was a respectable, well-bred man.

"Those your children?" asked the proprietor.

"My son and daughter."

"You driving to the country for them?"

"To Walla Walla Camp, in Maine. There are two camps alongside one another, one for boys and the other for girls. Mrs. Keane has charge of the girls, while her husband, Hector, who looks like an old boy scout..."

The proprietor was listening with care, not to him, but to his radio, his heavy eyebrows knitted, and fiddling with the knobs to try and get better reception, glaring at the juke-box, the noise of which drowned the other sound.

"...has managed, it is not known how, to slip through three successive police road blocks, and at about eleven o'clock was reported seen on Highway 2, driving north in a stolen car..."

"Who's that?" asked Steve.

The radio continued:

"Be careful! He is armed."

Then:

"Our next news bulletin will be broadcast at two o'clock."

Music followed.

"Who's that?"

Steve was being insistent, for no reason.

"The guy who escaped from Sing Sing and shut the little girl in a closet with a chocolate bar."

"What little girl?"

"Farmer's daughter, at Croton Lake."

Preoccupied, the proprietor paid no further attention to him, looking around for someone more or less sober to talk to. He went toward a corner table where two men and two women sat drinking beer, elderly people, who looked as if they might be building contractors and their wives.

The music prevented Steve from hearing what was said. The proprietor pointed to the vacant stool beside him, and one of the women, the one nearer the cigarette machine, seemed suddenly to remember something. The proprietor listened, nodding his head; he gazed uncertainly at the telephone on the wall, and finally came back to Steve Hogan.

"You didn't notice anything?"

"Notice what?"

"You didn't see if he was tattooed on one wrist?"

Steve didn't follow, was doing his best to grasp what was wanted of him.

"Who?"

"The man you bought a drink for."

"He didn't drink it. No offense."

At this the proprietor shrugged his shoulders and looked at him in a way he disliked. Now that he probably wouldn't be served with any more drink, and since there was no one to talk to, he might as well go.

He put a five-dollar bill on the counter, right in the wettest place, climbed off his stool unsteadily, and said:

"Keep the change!"

At the same time he made sure no one was giving him any dirty looks. He wouldn't have stood for it.

3

As HE WENT toward the door, walking nonchalantly, as though in slow motion, his lips wore the benevolent, protective smile of a strong man fallen among weaklings. He felt like a giant. Two men talking with their backs to him and their heads close together stood in the way, so he swept them aside with a grand gesture, and though they were both as tall as he was, he had the impression of overtopping them by a head. In any case, the men made no protest. Steve was not looking for a fight, with them, or with anyone, and if, when he reached the door, he turned and stood motionless, looking back into the room, he did not do so as a challenge.

He took time to light a cigarette and he felt fine. The air outside was fine too, pleasantly cool; the pretentious roadhouse next door, with the row of lights outlining its gable, was ridiculous; the cars passed along the smooth surface of the road, all making the same sound. He went to his own car, which he had left in the darker part of the parking lot, and opened the door; and all his movements, which were of a surprising largeness, everything he saw, everything he did gave him an inward satisfaction.

As he slid behind the wheel he saw the man, sitting where Nancy should have been. Despite the darkness he instantly recognized the long oval of the face, the deep-set eyes, and he was dismayed neither by finding him there nor by all that his presence implied.

Instead of drawing back, hesitating, perhaps adopting a defensive attitude, he arranged himself comfortably, pulling up his trousers as he ordinarily did, then reached out to slam the door, and turned the safety catch.

He did not wait for the man to speak, and said, more in a conversational tone than as though he were asking a question:

"It's you?"

The words had not their ordinary meaning. He was living several layers above everyday reality, in a sort of superreality, and he expressed himself in abbreviations, sure of himself and sure of being understood.

In saying, "It's you?" he was not simply asking if this was the man to whom he had offered a drink in the bar, and the other made no mistake about it. The question really meant:

"It's you they're looking for?"

In his own mind it comprised even more. He could not have explained it, but in the few words he gathered together the scattered images collected almost unconsciously in the course of the evening, and assembled them in a coherent whole, luminous with simplicity.

He was proud of his subtlety, proud of his calm, of the way he thrust the ignition key into its slot without a tremor of his hand, awaiting, before he turned it, his companion's reply.

No humility. He did not want to appear humble. No indignation, either, such as the proprietor of the bar might have shown, or a woman of Nancy's type. And no panic. He wasn't afraid. He understood. The proof that the other also understood and respected him in his turn was that he answered simply, without protest, without denial, without evasion:

"They recognized me?"

This was the way he had always imagined a dialogue between two men, real men, coming together on the highways. No unnecessary words. Every sentence meaning as much as a long speech. Nearly everyone talks too much. Had Steve needed to make any speeches earlier in the evening, to get the man in the first bar to see that he was something more than the commonplace office worker he might have looked?

And now another stranger had chosen to take refuge in his car. He was armed, the radio had just said. But did he feel the need to point his gun at him? Did he seem threatening?

"I think the owner's suspicious," Steve told him.

It was queer the way things that he hadn't registered were coming back to him. He knew perfectly well that this was a man who had escaped from Sing Sing. He didn't remember the name, but then he could never remember names, only figures, and above all telephone numbers. A name ending in "gan," like his own.

There had been something about a farmer's wife near a lake, and a little girl locked in a closet with a bar of chocolate. He could recall the little girl's picture clearly, and so far as he could remember it was the first time he had ever seen a photograph projected on to a television screen.

Then there had been a picture of a smashed shop-window, and some talk of Highway Two. Right?

If he'd been drunk, how could he have remembered all that?

"What description did they give?"

"They said something about tattoo marks."

He went on waiting, without impatience, for the signal to start his engine and it was as though he had known all his life that this hour would come. He was pleased, not only with the trust placed in him, but with the way he was bearing himself.

Hadn't he said earlier that this was his night?

"Are you able to drive?"

By way of reply he started off, asking:

"Shall I pass Providence on the country roads?"

"Stick to the highway."

"And suppose the police..."

The young man reached over into the back of the car,

picked up Steve's brown checked sports coat and straw hat, which were on the seat. The jacket was too wide at the shoulders, but he huddled in his corner like a traveler asleep, with the hat pulled over his eyes.

"Don't exceed the speed limit."

"Check."

"And don't try to go through red lights."

So as not to have the cops after them, of course.

He was the one who asked:

"What is your name again?"

"Sid Halligan. They've given it out often enough over the air."

"Well, Sid, suppose we come to a road block..."

He drove at forty-five, like the family cars they could see, piled high with baggage.

"Follow the others."

He had never been in a situation like this before, and yet he had no need of explanations. He felt as clearheaded as that first stranger, the one with blue eyes who resembled him.

First, on a night like this they couldn't stop all the cars on all the roads in New England and examine the passengers one by one without causing the biggest bottleneck of all time. Probably all they were doing was to have a quick glance inside the cars, more especially the ones occupied by a man alone.

In his car they were two.

"It's a laugh!" he thought.

Later on, past Providence, he'd strike up a conversation again. He had been right, after all, not to be annoyed by his companion's silence in the bar. Didn't he talk to Steve naturally, like an old friend?

He had to watch the road. The cars coming the other way were more numerous. Crossroads were now beginning to appear frequently, and on a lower level could be seen the lights of a big town.

"Sure you know the way?" said the voice in the shadow.

"I've done it at least ten times."

"If there's a road block——"

"I know. You told me."

"I suppose you can guess what would happen if you took it into your head to . . ."

Why did he have to say that? He didn't have to keep his hand in his pocket, either, probably resting on the butt of his gun.

"I won't talk."

"Fine."

He would have been disappointed if there had been no road block. Every time he saw stationary lights he thought it had happened, but in the end it turned out to be quite different from what he had imagined. The cars began to close up on one another until they were touching, and finally they came to a stop. There were stopped cars as far ahead as one could see, and they'd move forward a few yards only to stop again, as in a queue.

"This is it!"

"Yeah."

"Nervous?"

He regretted the word, which brought forth no reply. Once when they stopped opposite a bar he was tempted to dash in and have a quick one, but he didn't dare to suggest it.

Despite the coolness of the evening he began to sweat unpleasantly, and his fingers drummed on the steering wheel. Sometimes Halligan was buried in darkness, then, because of the lights of a roadhouse or filling station, he would be glaringly visible, motionless in his corner like a man asleep. Despite his long, narrow face his head must be bigger than it looked, for the straw hat was not too large for him and Steve had a big head himself.

"Cigarette?"

"No."

Steve lit one. His hand trembled like that of the man in the first bar when he had lit his, but with him he was sure it was just nervousness, or, rather, impatience. He wasn't scared. Just in a hurry to get it over with.

He could now see the way the road block was organized. White-painted hurdles set up across the road allowed only a single file of cars to pass in either direction and this caused a bottleneck, but the cars did not actually stop at the barrier; they just slowed right down while uniformed police had a quick look inside.

Past Providence it would no doubt be over because they probably didn't search so far.

"What was that about the little girl?"

The radio was going in the car in front of them, and a woman had her head on the driver's shoulder.

Halligan made no reply. Not the right time to ask. Steve would broach the subject later. He also intended to go on with what he had been saying in the log cabin. If a man like Sid couldn't understand, no one could.

Had Sid always been like this? Had it come to him naturally, without any effort? Most likely he'd been very poor. If you were raised in a crowded slum, the whole family living in one room, and were a member of a gang by the time you were ten, it was bound to be easier.

Maybe he didn't even realize?

"Keep going."

And as they stopped again: "How much gas in the tank?"

"Half full."

"How many miles does that mean?"

"About a hundred and fifty."

This was when he could have done with a rye to keep him on the level he had attained. Every now and then the well-being, the assurance threatened to vanish; stark, unpleasant thoughts occurred to him, like the notion, for instance, that if they were arrested together the police would not believe in his innocence, and relays of detectives would grill him for hours without allowing him a glass of water or a cigarette. They'd take away his necktie and his shoelaces. They'd bring Nancy to identify him.

When there were only three cars left ahead his legs became so weak that it took him a moment to find the accelerator when they had to move on.

"See you don't let them smell your breath."

Halligan spoke out of the corner of his mouth without moving, still looking like a man asleep.

Their car reached the barrier, and as Steve was about to pull up a policeman signed to him to keep moving, to go faster, merely giving a vague glance inside. It was all over. It was over. The highway was clear ahead of them, or, rather, the road leading down to the town through which they had to pass.

"Done it!" exclaimed Steve with relief, accelerating to forty.

"Done what?"

"We got through."

"The sign said thirty-five miles an hour. To Boston. You know the way?"

"It's the way I always go."

They passed a restaurant festooned with red lights, and it made him thirsty; once again, however, he didn't mention it and lit a cigarette instead.

"Hey, what are you doing?"

"Why?"

"You're driving, aren't you? Can't you keep to the right?"

"Sorry!"

It was true that all of a sudden he was driving a little wildly; he couldn't tell why. Up to the time when they had passed the barrier he had felt well under control, as steady and sure of himself as when he'd left the log cabin. But now his body was inclined to sag, and the road ahead of him seemed to lack substance. At one turning he nearly went onto the sidewalk.

His thoughts had also grown confused, and he resolved that when they got back on the highway he would ask Sid's permission to stop for a drink. Would Sid mistrust him? Hadn't he just proved himself?

"Are you sure you're on the right road?"

"I saw an arrow marked Boston a little way back."

Then with a sudden disquiet:

"Where are you going?"

"Farther on. Don't worry."

"I'm on my way to Maine. My wife's waiting for me with the children."

"Keep going."

They had left the outer districts behind, and now there was nothing but darkness on either side of the highway, along which the cars, few and far between, traveled at an increasing speed.

"You'll have to fill her up before the gas stations close."

Steve assented. He wanted to ask his companion a question, just one:

"Do you trust me?" He would have liked Sid to trust him, to know that Steve would never let him down.

Instead of this he said:

"Most men are scared."

"Of what?" the other muttered. He had pulled off the hat and was lighting a cigarette.

Steve groped around for an answer. He ought to have been able to find one in a single word, because those are the only real answers. The thing seemed to him so clear that he was enraged by his inability to explain himself.

"I don't know," he confessed finally.

But he added instantly, feeling that it was a stroke of genius:

"They don't know it, either!"

Sid Halligan wasn't scared. Perhaps he had never been scared, and that was why Steve respected him.

This guy, not even well built, was alone on the highway, most likely without a cent in his pocket, and the police of three states had been chasing him for the last forty-eight hours.... He had no wife or children or home, probably no friends, either, and he went his way in the night, when he had needed a gun he smashed a shopwindow to get one.

Did he ever wonder what people thought of him? He had leaned with his elbows on the bar, not drinking the glass of beer in front of him, waiting for the chance to move on, ready to clear out in an instant if the radio broadcast his description again and people started to look suspiciously at him.

"How long were you in for, at Sing Sing?"

Halligan started, not at the question, but because he had been on the verge of falling asleep and Steve's voice had aroused him.

"Ten years."

"How many had you done?"

"Four."

"You must have gone in pretty young!"

"Nineteen."

"And before that?"

"Three years in a reform school."

"What for?"

"Stolen cars."

"And the ten-year stretch?"

"A car and a holdup."

"In New York?"

"On the road."

"Where were you coming from?"

"Missouri."

"Did you use your gun?"

"If I'd fired they'd have sent me to the chair."

Once, a year before, Steve had very nearly witnessed a holdup, in broad daylight on Madison Avenue. To be precise, he had seen the epilogue. Opposite his office there was a bank with an imposing doorway. Shortly after nine in the morning, when he was putting through his first phone calls to the airports, the clangorous ringing of a bell had sounded outside, the bank's alarm bell; and the people in the street had stood stock-still, most of the traffic had stopped, a policeman in uniform had run toward the doorway, pulling his revolver out of its holster.

After an absurdly short time he had reappeared, accompanied by one of the uniformed bank police, and they were pushing in front of them two men who were so young that they were almost children, and whose wrists were handcuffed, and who held their arms in front of their faces. Someone had dashed out of a photographer's store and started taking snapshots, and as though by magic, as though the whole thing had been rehearsed, a police car had pulled up at the edge of the sidewalk, its siren going full blast.

For about two minutes the two youths had stayed there, isolated from the crowd, alone in the middle of a cleared space, motionless, in the same attitude, with the solemn doorway of the bank for a background: and when at length they were taken away Steve had reflected that it would be at least ten years before they again saw a city street, a sidewalk. What had most struck him, he remembered, was the thought that during all that time they would be deprived of women.

The picture of the little girl in the closet troubled him because she made him think of Bonnie, although Bonnie was ten years old.

"Why did you shut her in there?"

"Because she was yelling and she'd have roused the neighbors. I had to give myself time to get away from the village. I didn't want to tie her up like her mother, in case I hurt her. I found a chocolate bar in the drawer and I gave it to her, then I pushed her in the closet and told her not to be scared and locked her in. I wasn't rough with her. I did my best not to scare her."

"What about her mother?"

"There's a garage that's still open. You'd better stop and fill up."

Automatically Halligan thrust his hand in his pocket after putting the hat back on his head and huddling in his corner.

"Got enough dough?"

"Yes."

"Well, hurry up."

Without looking at them the garage hand started to unscrew the cap on the tank.

"How much?"

"Fill it up."

They sat silent and motionless. Then Steve held out a ten-dollar bill.

"You wouldn't happen to have any cold beer?"

Sid, in his corner, could say nothing.

"No beer. But I might hunt up a pint of hooch."

As his hand grasped the flat bottle Steve was so terrified in case Sid should prevent his drinking that he uncorked it instantly, and gulped down as much of the liquid as he could manage at a single breath.

"Thanks, pal. Keep the change."

"You going far?"

"Maine."

"The traffic begins to ease up this time of night."

They started off again. After a moment Steve said:

"You want some?"

And his voice, as he asked the question, was the same as if he had been speaking to Nancy; as if he felt guilty, or thought it necessary to apologize. Halligan didn't answer. He probably didn't drink. For one thing it would have been dangerous for him to get drunk. Besides he didn't need to.

Why not explain this to him? Steve felt no self-consciousness. They had time enough. The road stretched far ahead of them, bordered, so far as one could judge, by forests.

"Don't you ever get drunk?"

"No."

"Does it make you feel bad?"

"I just don't feel like it."

"Because you don't feel the need," said Steve.

He glanced at his companion and saw that he did not understand. He must be overwhelmed with fatigue. Here in the car he looked even paler than he had in the log cabin, and he must be keeping a tight hold on himself so as not to fall asleep. Had he so much as closed his eyes since he broke out of the prison?

"Have you slept?"

"No."

"Are you sleepy?"

"I'll sleep later."

"Generally, I don't drink either. Just one with my wife at the end of the day, whenever we go home together. Other evenings I don't have the time, on account of the children."

He had a notion he had already told about the children waiting for him and Ida, the colored girl, standing by the door with her hat already on her head, looking as though she thought he'd got home late on purpose. Or was it something he had just thought about? Now that he had a bottle handy he felt fine.

He groped on the seat with one hand, not to have a drink but just to make sure it was still there; and his companion's voice out of the darkness said sharply:

"No!"

Sid was even more emphatic than Nancy.

"Keep your eyes on the road!"

"I'm watching it."

"You're driving all over the place."

"Do you want me to go faster?"

"I want you to drive straight."

"You don't trust me? I drive best when I've had a drink."

"One, maybe."

"I'm not drunk."

Sid shrugged his shoulders, sighed in the manner of a man not disposed to argue. Steve fumed silently. This attitude humiliated him, and he began to wonder whether Sid was intelligent.

Why did he let him drive instead of taking the wheel himself if he didn't trust him? The answer occurred to him instantly, which proved that the mouthful of whiskey he had gulped at the garage had not impaired his reasoning powers.

Even if they didn't run into another road block, there was always a chance that a patrol would hold them up to check his license. The police would automatically go to the driver's side, so they would take no more notice of the man asleep in the other corner than they had done outside Providence.

It was beginning to get cold. The air was damp. The dashboard clock had not worked for months, and for some reason Steve did not like to get his watch out of his pocket. He had no idea of the time. When he tried to work out how much time had passed he became muddled, opened his mouth to say something, and then closed it again.

He didn't know what he had been going to say. If he could stop a minute he'd get his raincoat, which must be either in the back of the car or in the trunk, because he was beginning to shiver with only his shirt on, and he could not very well ask for his jacket.

"Where are you heading for?"

He shouldn't have asked that question, which might arouse Halligan's distrust. Luckily, Sid did not hear, for despite his efforts he had fallen asleep at last, and from his half-open mouth came a sound of regular breathing, with a slight wheeze.

Groping on the seat with his right hand, Steve found the bottle and cautiously pulled out the cork with his teeth. Since it was pretty certain that he would not be allowed to drink again, he drained it to the last drop, in three gulps, holding his breath, while a sudden heat rose to his temples, and misted his eyes.

He took care to put back the cork and replace the bottle, and he was just raising his hand from the seat when the car skidded violently, then gave several lurches. He straightened it out in time, took his foot off the accelerator, steadily pushed down the brake, and after a few more jerks, pulled up at the side of the road.

He was so taken aback, the thing had been so unexpected and so quick, that he had not paid any attention to Sid, and was dumfounded to find that he was pointing his gun at him. Sid's face was expressionless save for the look of an animal recoiling to meet a threat.

"A tire..." stammered Steve, while sweat broke out on his forehead.

It was not so much because of the revolver. It was because he could scarcely speak. His tongue had become so thick that the word was distorted as it issued from his lips. He tried again.

"A blowout... not on purpose..."

Without saying anything or lowering his weapon, Halligan lit up the dashboard, picked up the bottle, which he held against the light with a look of disgust, and tossed it out of the window.

"Get out."

"O.K."

He would never have believed that alcohol could have such a devastating effect on him. Having got the door open, he was obliged to hang on to it while he got out.

"Do you have a spare?"

"In the trunk."

"Well, make it fast."

With legs at once stiff and wobbly he worked his way along

to the back of the car, but he was now certain that if he tried to go on standing he would end by collapsing altogether. It was particularly dangerous to bend down, because of dizziness. Even the handle of the trunk was too difficult, too complicated for him, and it was Halligan who came and opened it.

"Got a jack?"

"I should have."

"Where?"

He didn't know. He didn't know anything any more. Something had given way inside him. He wanted to sit down on the grass at the edge of the road and start to cry.

"Well?"

He had to keep going whatever happened. If he didn't show he was co-operative Halligan was quite capable of killing him. A car passed every two or three minutes, but the rest of the time they were alone in space, with the branches of trees rustling softly above their heads.

The people who went by, nearly all driving very fast, took no notice of the car pulled up at the side of the road, or of the two figures of which they caught a momentary glimpse in the beams of their headlights.

Halligan could shoot him if he felt like doing so, and drag his body into the woods, where it might not be found for days, particularly if they were at some distance from the nearest village. Would he hesitate to kill anyone? Probably not. Earlier, talking of the little girl, he had said that he had not hurt her, and hadn't wanted to frighten her. But what had he done to the mother? Steve no longer dared to put the question to him, or any question.

He had the jack in his hand. It was the right rear tire that was flat, and Sid stood near him, holding his gun.

"You wondering where to put it?"

"I know."

To avoid bending over, he went down on all fours, trying to

put the jack in place, and suddenly he felt himself give way; he sprawled limply on the ground arms outstretched, murmuring:

"Sorry."

He did not pass out. In fact, if Halligan hadn't been standing over him with the gun the sensation would not have been unpleasant. Everything in him had gone slack all at once. It was as though his body and head had emptied and he didn't have to make any more effort, it was useless, he had nothing to do but let go and wait.

Perhaps he was going to sleep? It didn't matter. He had only once before been in this state, one night when they had had a party at home and he had drunk off all the dregs. When he and Nancy were alone he had let himself flop into an armchair, his legs thrust out in front of him, and he had sighed with intense relief, a blissful smile on his lips:

"Fin-ished!"

Although he knew what followed largely from what his wife had told him, he had a feeling he'd nonetheless retained certain lazy recollections. She had made him drink some coffee, most of which he had spilled, and then she had made him sniff ammonia. She had helped him to his feet, talking sharply in a commanding voice, and since he kept falling back she had ended by dragging him with his arms over her shoulders and his feet trailing on the carpet.

"I didn't want the children to find you sprawling in a chair in the living room when they got up in the morning...."

She had managed to undress him and put on his pajamas.

"Lift yourself up, Steve. Do you hear me? Your hips, not your shoulders."

Halligan was now dragging him off the side of the road, where he let him slump on the long grass. Steve's eyes were not closed. He wasn't asleep. He knew what was going on, could hear Sid swearing as he wound up the jack, which squeaked.

There was no sense in worrying because in any case he was

at his mercy. Defenseless as a newborn babe. The expression amused him. He repeated it to himself several times. Defenseless! It was all he could do to get himself seated upright when he realized that his head was resting on some nettles.

"Don't move!"

He made no attempt to answer. He knew he couldn't speak—and that was a laugh! He could still move his lips, with some effort, and no more sound came than out of a choked whistle.

Hadn't he said this was his night? Too bad Nancy wasn't there to see! True enough, she wouldn't have understood. Anyway, if she'd been there nothing would have happened. By this time they would have reached the camp.

He didn't know the time. He no longer needed to know. Nancy would have hesitated to wake Mrs. Keane. Her first name was Gertrude. You could hear Mr. Keane shouting to her right across the camp:

"Gertrude!"

They had no children. It was impossible, he didn't know why, to imagine those two in the act of making a child.

Hector Keane wore khaki shorts which made him look like an overgrown boy, and he always carried a little trumpet slung round his neck for calling the children together. He joined in all their games, climbed trees, and one knew that it wasn't just to earn his living, or from a sense of duty, but because he really enjoyed it.

Sid was still working furiously on the wheel, and that was a laugh too, because it made him mad and he kept on muttering things under his breath.

Did he want to kill Steve? Anyway it wouldn't get him anywhere, only get him sent to the chair sooner or later, to use his own expression.

Perhaps he was going to leave him here. Steve wished he had put on his raincoat, because he was beginning to shiver.

If he could manage to stay awake, perhaps he'd start getting some strength back. Despite the heaviness of his head, he refused to close his eyes, and he wasn't losing consciousness. If his tongue hadn't felt so thick, as though paralyzed, he'd have been capable of repeating everything he had said since the start of the evening. Maybe not in the same order. That remained to be seen!

He was sure he had made sense. It might not seem that way at first, because he hadn't always bothered to use ordinary sentences. He had used short cuts. He had seemed to mix the subjects.

Actually it all added up, and he didn't regret a thing. Only his raincoat. And also not having asked when he might have what had happened to the mother of the little girl. He was sure Sid would have told him. The way things were, Sid had no reason to hide anything from him. Anyway, it had been given out over the radio.

Maybe Nancy was still in the bus. What would she do when she got to Hampton? There was still about twenty miles of bad road along the shore to reach the camp. If she couldn't get a cab, and if, as was probable, all the hotels in Hampton were full, what would she do?

In order to move more freely Sid had taken off the tweed jacket, and he was now fitting on the spare wheel. When he had finished the job he closed the trunk without bothering to put in the wheel with the flat tire. After all, it wasn't his car!

Steve was curious to see what he would do next. He seemed uncertain, worried; he put on the jacket again and came toward Steve. Standing over him, he stared down at him for some moments, then, bending down, he slapped him on either cheek, without anger, as though perfunctorily.

"Can you get up now?"

Steve had no wish to get up. The slaps had scarcely ruffled his blissful torpor, and he gazed upward with an indifferent eye.

"Try!"

Gently he shook his head and when he raised his arms to protect himself it was too late, two more slaps had stung his face.

"Now?"

He got on all fours, then to his knees, and his lips moved with the soundless words:

"Don't beat me!"

Why did he think of the little girl and smile?

It was a laugh. With Halligan's help he staggered to the car and collapsed on the seat, but not behind the steering wheel.

4

BEFORE he opened his eyes he wondered at finding himself motionless. He did not yet remember the journey in the car, or the place he might be, but some obscure instinct told him that this stillness was unnatural, even alarming.

Perhaps he made a slight movement and he felt an acute pain at the nape of the neck, like a thousand needles being driven into the flesh; and he thought he must have been injured, which would account for the heaviness of his head.

At the same time through his closed eyelids he perceived the glow of sunlight.

He could have sworn he had not slept, and he was all the more baffled by the gap in his memory in that he had never lost the sense of the car.

Yet the movement had ceased. He was either injured or ill, and he was afraid to learn the truth, which could only be unpleasant; he postponed the moment of facing it, trying to plunge back into his torpor.

He was on the verge of succeeding, the torpor was creeping over him again, when a horn sounded close at hand, so piercing that he thought he had never heard anything like it, and a car went screaming past. Almost immediately there followed a truck with a hanging chain that bounced along the road with a sound of jingling bells.

He even thought he could hear real bells very far off, farther away than the twittering of birds and the piping of a blackbird, but this must surely be an illusion, as no doubt was his imagining a sky of unreal blue in which two gleaming white clouds were suspended.

Was the scent of the sea and of pine trees also an illusion? And a rustling in the grass, which he took to be the movement of a squirrel?

His groping hand expected to feel smooth grass, but encountered instead the worn cloth upholstery of the car.

He opened his eyes suddenly, in defiance, and was dazzled by the light of the most brilliant morning he had ever known.

Except when cars passed, each setting up a scurry of cool air, there was no sound other than the singing of the birds and it moved him to discover that the squirrel really was there, now halfway up the bronze trunk of a pine tree and watching him with small, bright, round eyes.

The warmth of a summer's day rose up from the earth in a mist that caused the light to quiver, and the light so penetrated him through his eyes that he felt giddy and the sickening aftertaste of whiskey rose in his mouth!

There was no one in the car but himself, and he was not where he had been when he got in, but was seated at the wheel. The road was wide, smooth, splendid, built as though for the triumph of an emperor, with its white lines defining three lanes of traffic in either direction, pinewoods extending on either side as far as the eye could see, and the blue sky becoming mother-of-pearl over to the right, where perhaps, not very far away, the white fringe of the sea rolled up onto the beach.

When he tried to straighten his huddled body the same pain shot through the side of his neck nearer the open door, and he had no need to run his hand over the skin to know that he was not injured. He was simply stiff with cold. His shirt was still limp with the dampness of the night. He fished in his pocket for a cigarette, lighted it, and found the taste so unpleasant that he hesitated to smoke it. If he did so it was because the mere act of putting it to his lips, inhaling the smoke, and blowing it out again in a familiar movement gave him the feeling of having returned to life.

Before getting out he waited for a break between the cars that were passing at a steady rhythm, unlike that of the day before out of New York, and also unlike that of the night. These cars nearly all bore Massachusetts license plates, and the people in them wore light-colored clothes, the men in gaudy shirts and the women in shorts and some in swim suits. He saw golf bags, and canoes on the roofs.

They probably came from Boston and were heading for the nearby beaches. The radio was no doubt triumphantly heralding a perfect weekend, and predicting, as happened every year, that a million and a half New Yorkers would crowd Coney Island beach during the afternoon.

Despite the mildness of the air, he felt cold inside, and he searched fruitlessly for his tweed jacket or his raincoat. He had another, lighter jacket in his suitcase. Going around to the back of the car, he opened the trunk, and his expression became one of stupefaction and dismay.

He was filled with a vast sadness that morning, an almost cosmic sadness. The suitcase was gone, but before its removal Nancy's things had been taken out of it—underclothing, sandals, and a swim suit lay scattered among the tools. The toilet kit, which contained among other things his comb, toothbrush, and razor, was also gone.

He did not attempt to think. He was just sad, and would have given a great deal to have things turn out less squalidly.

Only when he had shut the trunk did he notice that the right-hand rear tire was flat. Until then he had not wondered why the car was drawn up on the grass.

There had been another blowout, on the same wheel as before, which was not very surprising since the spare tire was old and he hadn't remembered to have it pumped up.

He had heard nothing. Halligan had not troubled to wake him, or else had tried and been unable to do so. Why should he have awakened him? He had gone off with the suitcase after ridding it of its feminine contents, and, to make the look of the car pulled up at the side of the road seem natural, he had taken the precaution of placing Steve behind the wheel.

Perhaps there was a local bus stop somewhere near. Or else he could have thumbed a ride. The suitcase would have inspired confidence.

At the farthest point along the road, on the horizon, a red roof was visible in the sunshine, and the things gleaming below it must be a row of gasoline pumps. It was a long way off, half a mile or more. Feeling incapable of walking so far, Steve stationed himself beside the immobilized car, and, turning leftward, extended his arm to every vehicle that passed.

Five or six went by without stopping. Then a red oil truck slowed, and the driver signed to him to jump on to the running board, opening the door without pulling up entirely.

"Flat?"

"Yes. Is that a garage down there?"

"Looks like it."

Steve felt himself grow pale. The jolting of the truck made him feel sick, his head hurt as though it had been hit with a hammer.

"Are we far from Boston?" he asked.

The huge, redheaded driver glanced at him with astonishment in which there was a hint of suspicion.

"You going to Boston?"

"Well, no, I'm going to Maine."

"Boston's fifty miles back. Right now we're going through New Hampshire."

They were approaching the red-roofed building, which was indeed a garage, and near it was a cafeteria.

"I guess you could do with a cup of coffee and then some!"

It must be obvious that he had a hangover. The people passing in the cars had all slept in their beds, the men were newly shaven, wore clean linen.

He felt dirty, even inside. He had still not regained full control of his movements, and when he grasped the door to get down he was ashamed to see that his hands were shaking.

"Good luck!"

"Thanks."

He had not even offered him a cigarette. Perhaps he would have felt his position less acutely if it had still been raining, with the sky gray and windy. Even the garage was new, meticulously clean, with attendants in white overalls. He went up to one who was doing nothing.

"My car's stopped a little way back," he said in a voice so dismal that he must have sounded like a beggar.

"Better see the boss in the office."

He had to pass an open car in which three youths and three girls in shorts were already eating ice-cream cones. They stared at his disheveled figure. His beard had grown. When he entered the office, in a corner of which new tires were stacked, the proprietor, in shirt sleeves, smoking a cigar, waited for him to speak.

"My car's stopped half a mile back on the way to Boston. Flat tire."

"You don't have a spare?"

He chose to say no rather than confess that he had left it by the roadside.

"I'll send someone. It'll take at least an hour."

He saw a phone booth, but decided to wait until he'd had some coffee.

He did not blame Sid Halligan for clearing out, realizing that the man had had no choice. What rankled was the disappointment he felt.

Looking at it more closely, he perceived that it was of himself he was really ashamed, above all of the fragments of recollection that were now returning to him, that he would have liked to blot out forever.

"Have you the key?"

"It's on the dashboard."

As he said this he realized that he had no idea whether the key was there or not, since he had not been the last person to drive. What if Halligan had taken it with him or thrown it away in the bushes?

"I suppose you'll wait next door?"

"Yes. I've been driving all night."

"New York?"

"Yes."

Did the man's slight grimace mean that a whole night was a long time to come up from New York, and that Steve must have stopped a good many times on the way?

Steve was glad to get out of the office.

"You and me, Sid—we're brothers...!"

It was these words, which he had repeated like a leitmotiv, that now shamed him. At that time he had been sprawled in his corner in the darkness, probably smiling beatifically and proclaiming to his companion that he was happier than he had ever been in his life....

Perhaps he had talked less than he imagined? In any case he had thought he was talking, in a slow, sodden voice, his tongue stiff and too big for his mouth.

"Brothers... You don't know what I mean, do you?"

Why, when he had been drinking, did he invariably suppose no one could understand him? Was it because things buried in the depths of his being, of which he knew nothing and in everyday life preferred to know nothing, then came to the surface to surprise and alarm him?

He preferred to think not. It was not possible. He had talked about Nancy. He had thought a great deal about her, not like a husband or a man in love, but like a superior being from whom no secret of human nature is concealed.

"She lives the kind of life she wanted, the kind she decided to live. Who cares if I..."

He was reluctant to enter the cafeteria, to be examined again from head to foot. There was a big horseshoe counter with fixed stools and chrome-nickel appliances for cooking and making coffee. Two families were seated at tables in the bay window, both with children, one of them a little girl Bonnie's age, and the smell of bacon and eggs filled the air.

"Do you want breakfast?"

He had seated himself at the counter. The waitresses wore uniforms and white caps. There were three of them, fresh, pretty girls.

"Give me some coffee first!"

He had to telephone the camp, but he dared not do it right away. Glancing up, he was astonished to see by the electric clock that it was eight.

"Is it going?" he asked.

The girl answered gaily:

"What time did you think it was? Maybe you figure it's still last night?"

Everyone looked so clean! The mingled odor of coffee and bacon and eggs had a tang of their house in Scottville on a spring morning, with the sunshine streaming into the breakfast nook. They had no dining room. A shoulder-high partition divided the kitchen in two. It was more cozy. The children came down to breakfast in pajamas, eyes still gummy with sleep, and the little boy had a quaint look, as though his face had faded during the night. His sister would say:

"You look like a Chinaman!"

"And you?... You look like—like..." He always searched for a proper comeback and never found one.

It was clean and bright at home too. It was gay. Where had

he got all that stuff he had talked, or thought he had talked, to Halligan?

During that time he had seen nothing of him except a profile, a cigarette hanging from the lower lip, which he replaced as soon as it was finished, as though he were afraid of falling asleep.

"You're a man, Sid—a real man!"

That profile had seemed to him the most impressive in the world.

"You could have killed me just now."

The worst thing was that he seemed to remember that several times a disdainful voice had rasped:

"Shut up!"

So it was true he had talked, however laboriously, however indistinctly.

"You could have abandoned me at the side of the road. If you didn't do it because you were scared I'd give you away to the cops, you were wrong. You got me wrong. It hurts to think you got me wrong!"

He had to grit his teeth, in order not to cry out in anger, in fury. This, all this, was Steve Hogan! It had come from nowhere but himself!

"I know I don't look like it, but me too, I'm a man. . . ."

A man! A man! A man! It had been an obsession. Was he so terrified of not being one? He had mixed everything up—the tracks, the highway, his wife going off by coach.

"It was a good lesson I taught her!"

He was mechanically stirring his scalding coffee.

"When I came out of the bar and saw that note in the car. . ."

Sid had looked at him, and Steve was almost sure he had seen him smile. If so, it was his only smile that night.

He must not think about it any more or he'd be unable to call Nancy. He had still not decided what he was going to say. Would she believe him if he told the truth, supposing he had the courage to do so? What she was sure to do, knowing her as he did, was to ring up the police, if only in the hope of getting back the things Halligan had taken. She had a horror of losing anything, of being cheated in any way, and once she had made him go three miles to collect twenty-five cents change that a shop had failed to give her.

Perhaps he had told Sid about those twenty-five cents. He didn't know and didn't want to know. He sipped his coffee, and the hot liquid had an atrocious taste as it went down and it brought the acidity welling up into his throat. He had to swallow some ice water for fear of vomiting, and he took the precaution of looking round to see where the toilet was, in case he had to make a run for it.

He knew what he needed, but it was a remedy that frightened him. A shot of whiskey would fix him up in a moment. The trouble was, in an hour's time he would need another, and so it would go on.

"Have you found out if you're hungry or not?"

He tried to smile back.

"I guess I'm not."

She had understood. There was a knowing twinkle in the glance she gave him.

"The coffee won't stay down?"

"Hardly."

"If you want something else, there's a liquor store a hundred yards from here, behind the garage. That's the fourth time I've mentioned it this morning, and I don't even get a percentage!"

He was not the only one in his condition all along the highways, of course. There must be thousands, tens of thousands, who that morning were feeling uncomfortable inside their skins.

He put a coin on the counter, went out, found the way that led between two rows of pine trees to a group of houses. He would sooner have had a drink in a bar, sure that he would have stopped at that, but there was none nearby, so he had to buy a bottle.

"A half pint of whiskey."

"Scotch?"

Rye had too evil a memory for him to touch it again today.

"Three twenty-five."

His hand went to his left-hand trouser pocket and was suddenly motionless, like his gaze, because his wallet was no longer there. His face must have changed color, if such a thing was still possible.

The storekeeper asked:

"Anything wrong?"

"It's nothing. Something I left in the car."

"Your money?"

His other hand plunged into his right-hand pocket and he was somewhat reassured. He was in the habit of keeping one-dollar bills there, in a roll. Halligan had not searched that pocket, and Steve counted eight dollars. He would need money for the garage. But perhaps they would accept a check.

He thought it necessary to take shelter in the woods before drinking, and he took only two sips, just enough to straighten him up. It did him good at once, and he slipped the bottle into his pocket and tried another cigarette, which did not sicken him. As he turned he saw that he had not been mistaken earlier when he thought he could smell the sea: there it lay, calm and glittering between the dark green of the trees, with the red of a beach umbrella making a splash of color on a yellow strip of sand.

If he were questioned, what would he tell the police?

Gulls flew overhead, their white bellies gleaming in the blue of the sky, and he averted his gaze because they reminded him that Bonnie and Dan were waiting for him on another beach, less than seventy miles away. How had their mother explained his absence?

With his head bowed, he walked slowly toward the garage. There was no need now to worry about the police, because there was very little likelihood of their learning that he had driven Sid Halligan in his car.

The trouble with him was, he always found problems for himself. It was perfectly easy to explain the stolen suitcase and the other things. In any case he would be bound to admit that he had been drinking. Nancy already knew it. In two or three bars along the road—he wouldn't say exactly where—and when he had come out of one of them he had found the suitcase and the spare tire gone.

And that was that! It wasn't exactly pretty, and he wasn't particularly proud of himself. But after all, he didn't get drunk every day like his friend, Dick, whom Nancy nevertheless considered an interesting and even a superior type of man.

As for his telephoning so late, he would say that at the place where he had been held up with tire trouble the line had been damaged by the storm, and that it had only just been cleared. That's always happening.

He was nearly cheered up by his plan. One has to face facts. Everybody has to make small compromises with the truth, and pretty well every day of their lives. The sight of his car on the hydraulic lift in the garage was also reassuring. A mechanic was putting a new inner tube in the tire.

"This yours?" he asked, seeing Steve watching him.

"Yes."

"You drove quite a way after the blow-out."

Steve chose to say nothing.

"The boss wants to see you."

He went into the office.

"We've patched up your tire as well as we can. The car will be ready in a few minutes, if you want it. But if you're going any distance, I advise you not to leave it like that. There's a six-inch gash in the cover. We had to put in a new tube."

He was on the verge of ordering a new tire, with the idea of paying for it by check, when another consequence of the loss of his wallet suddenly dawned on him. Nobody along the way would accept a check without seeing some evidence of his identity. But his driver's license and all his other papers were in the wallet. Nor could he tell them to call up his bank, because it was Saturday. Until then, perhaps owing to the weather, he had kept on thinking it was Sunday.

"I'm not going far," he murmured.

As he entered the garage he had decided, after having a look at the car, to go and get something to eat. Now that the whiskey had settled his stomach he felt hungry. It would do him good to eat. He tried to figure how much money he would have left, and how much the repair and the new tube would cost.

Supposing he hadn't enough? Suppose they wouldn't let him take the car away?

"I'll be back in a few minutes."

"Suit yourself."

He would sooner telephone from the cafeteria; the garage proprietor made him feel uneasy, he didn't know why.

"Bacon and eggs this time?"

"Not yet. A cup of coffee."

He had some small change in his pocket. In the call box he dialed the operator and asked for Popham Beach 7, the Keanes' number. It took some time. He could hear his call being relayed from station to station, and all the voices sounded cheerful, as though the people on duty also felt that this was a special day.

If his wife were worried about him, she would very likely be keeping close to Gertrude Keane's office, and perhaps she would be the one to pick up the receiver. Turning to the wall, he raised the bottle to his lips for a quick sip of whiskey, just enough to clear his voice, which was more hoarse than usual.

"Walla Walla Camp speaking."

It was Mrs. Keane, who so resembled her own voice that he seemed to be able to see her at the other end of the line.

"This is Steve Hogan, Mrs. Keane."

"Why, good morning, Mr. Steve! Where are you? We expected you last night, as you said, and I left the key in the door of the bungalow."

It took him a moment to grasp what her words implied, yet he made himself ask, checking a growing panic:

"Is my wife there?"

"She isn't with you? Why no, Mr. Steve, she hasn't arrived here. Three families got here this morning, all from Boston. Hey, I can see your Bonnie at this moment, all sunburned and with her hair more blond than ever!"

"Tell me, Mrs. Keane, are you sure my wife isn't in the camp? She wouldn't have stopped off at the boys' camp?"

"No, my husband was here a few minutes ago, and he'd have told me. Where are you?"

He did not dare tell her that he didn't know. It hadn't occurred to him to ask the name of the nearest village.

"I'm on the road about seventy miles away. Do you know what time the bus gets to Hampton?"

"The night Greyhound?"

"Yes."

"It gets in at four in the morning. But you don't mean to say your wife . . . ?"

"Just a minute. If she'd arrived at Hampton at four in the morning, would she have been able to find any way of getting to you?"

"Why, yes. There's a connection on the local bus, which gets here at half-past five."

He didn't realize that he had pulled a dirty handkerchief out of his pocket to wipe the sweat off his forehead.

"Do you know the hotels in Hampton?"

"There are only two, the Maine and the Ambassador. I hope nothing's happened to her! Would you like me to call Bonnie?"

"Not just now."

"What should I tell her? She's looking through the window. She must have guessed I'm talking to you."

"Tell her we had car trouble and we'll be late."

"And if your wife arrives?"

"Tell her I called up, that everything's all right, and that I'll call again in a little while."

His hands were shaking; so were his knees. He dialed the operator again.

"Would you please get me the Maine Hotel, in Hampton."

After a few moments a voice said:

"Deposit thirty cents please."

He heard the coins drop.

"Maine Hotel."

"I want to know if a Mrs. Nancy Hogan checked in with you last night."

He had to repeat the name, spell it, and wait what seemed to him an interminable time.

"Would she have got here in the evening?"

"No—at four o'clock this morning on the Greyhound."

"Sorry. We didn't have anyone off the Greyhound."

Idiot! As though their hotel was so high-class that...

He wasted another thirty cents on a call to the Ambassador, where no one was registered in the name of Hogan and where the last traveler had checked in at twelve-thirty.

"You haven't heard anything about an accident to the Greyhound last night?"

"Nothing at all. We would have heard and it would have been in the papers. I've just read them. And anyway, the depot's right across the street, and..."

He had to leave the call box because he felt suffocated inside it. Even the waitress's smile hurt him. She couldn't know. She was gently teasing him.

"Made up your mind at last?"

How was he to find out what had happened to Nancy? He stared, unseeing, at his cup of coffee, and at that moment he loved his wife as he had never loved her; he would have given an arm, a leg, ten years of his life to have her there beside him, to beg her forgiveness, to beseech her to smile and be happy, to promise her that from now on she would always be happy.

She had gone off alone into the night, with nothing but her handbag, toward the lights at the crossroad, and he seemed to remember that it had been raining at the time. He imagined her tramping through the mud and being splashed by the cars streaming along the highway.

Had she been crying? Had the fact that he had felt the need to go and have a drink made her so unhappy? He had meant no harm when he took away the ignition key. It had been just tit-for-tat, almost a joke, because she had threatened to take the car on alone.

Would she really have done so?

He knew she was sensitive, despite appearances, but he was not always ready to admit it, particularly when he had had a drink or two.

"At times like this you hate me, don't you?"

He had sworn it wasn't so, that it was just a sort of momentary, childish rebellion.

"No; I know it! I can see it in your eyes. You look at me as though you regretted having tied your life to mine."

It wasn't true! He must find her at all costs, he must know what had happened to her. He wondered frantically where to turn next, still with the idea in mind, for no precise reason, that she had reached Hampton. He paid no attention to the puzzled gaze of the waitress.

"Give me change for a dollar."

He added, however, by way of explanation:

"I've got to telephone . . ."

As though she had read his thoughts, she asked jokingly:

"Have you lost someone?"

The question nearly caused him to burst into tears in front of her. She must have realized, because she added quickly, in an altered tone:

"I'm sorry!"

The switchboard operator already recognized his voice.

"What number do you want this time?"

"Police headquarters, Hampton, Maine."

"Do you want the County Police or the City Police?"

"City Police."

"Thirty cents, please."

He would never forget the sound of the coins dropping one by one into the box.

"Hampton City Police."

"I want to know if anything has happened to my wife, who should have arrived in Hampton on the Greyhound at four o'clock this morning."

"What name?"

"Hogan. Nancy Hogan."

"Age?"

"Thirty-four."

It was always a slight shock to him to realize that she was two years older than he.

"Description?"

He had an awful premonition. If they asked for Nancy's age and description, it was because they had picked up a body and wanted to make sure it was her before telling him.

"Medium height, light brown hair, wearing an almond-green suit and——"

"Nothing like that on the file."

"You're sure?"

"Certain. All we have here is an old biddy too drunk to stay on her feet, who says she was beaten up by a stranger and——"

"No one's been taken to the hospital?"

"One moment."

He checked the impulse to have another sip of whiskey. Absurdly enough, what restrained him was having the police at the other end of the line.

"A road accident, husband and wife. The husband's dead. It's not the same name."

"Nothing else?"

"Only an emergency appendectomy, a little girl. Local case. If it's anything that happened outside town you should call the sheriff's office."

"Thanks."

"You're welcome."

The switchboard operator made no pretense of not having heard the conversation.

"Shall I get you the sheriff's office?"

And as he grunted a vague affirmative:

"Thirty cents!"

The sheriff knew nothing about Nancy either. The Greyhound arrived without incident at its usual time, and had gone on ten minutes later.

He finally learned from the bus depot that no woman had got out at Hampton that night; and if he now took a gulp out of the bottle, turning toward the corner of the call box after making sure that the waitress wasn't looking, it was genuinely in the hope of controlling the shaking of his hands and knees. Before leaving the box he even called in a low voice, because no one could hear:

"Nancy!"

He did not know what to do next. If only he knew the name of the place where she had left him! He could remember the bar all right, and still more the fair-haired drunk who resembled him and whom he had thought of as a brother. Was there no way not to remember things like that just at this moment? He could also recall the stretch of road to the crossing, flanked by an open expanse on which he thought he had caught the outline of a factory, and more clearly, in a sort of village Main Street near the cafeteria, a bed draped with blue satin in the window of a furniture store.

It was somewhere on the way to Providence, but because of the circuitous route he had taken afterward he did not know whether it was twenty or fifty miles from there. He hadn't been worrying much about signposts just then! The world had been nothing but an endless highway with forty-five million motorists streaming at full speed past the red and blue lights of the bars. His night! he had bellowed with conviction.

"Bad news?"

He had returned to his seat, and he looked up at the waitress with the eyes of a lost child. She was no longer smiling. He could feel her sympathy. Slightly embarrassed at confiding in a young girl he did not know, he murmured:

"My wife."

"Accident?"

"I don't know. I'm trying to find out. Nobody can tell me."

"Where did it happen?"

"I don't know that, either. I don't even know what has happened. We started out from New York yesterday evening, happy, to get the children in Maine. Somewhere, for some reason or other, my wife decided to go on by bus."

His head lowered, he did not see that she was now gazing at him with more interest.

"Did you see her get on the bus?"

"No. I was in a bar about five hundred yards from the crossroad."

He had lost all sense of reticence. He had to talk to someone.

"You don't remember the name of the place?"

"No."

She realized why, but he didn't care. He would have made a public confession in the middle of the highway if anyone had asked him to.

"It was in Connecticut?"

"Before Providence, anyway. I think I'm going to hate that town all my life. I spent hours driving around it."

"What time of night?"

He made a helpless gesture.

"Does your wife have light-brown hair, and was she wearing a green suit with matching suède shoes?"

He raised his head so sharply that he felt a stab of pain in the back of his neck.

"How do you know?"

From under the counter she had picked up a copy of the local paper, and as he reached for it, he knocked over his coffeecup, which crashed on the floor.

"It doesn't matter."

Then she said quickly, to reassure him:

"She isn't dead. If it's her, she's out of danger."

The astonishing thing was that outside the garage, fifteen minutes ago, he had seen the truck bringing the Boston papers, had nearly bought one, then forgotten.

"On the back page," she said, leaning toward him. "That's where they put the latest news."

There were just a few lines under the heading:

"Unknown Woman Attacked on Highway."

5

A woman of about thirty, whose identity has not yet been established, was found unconscious by the roadside on Highway 3, near Pennichuck Crossroad, at about one o'clock this morning.

A head wound and the state of her clothes suggest that she was the victim of an assault. She was taken to Waterly Hospital, but it has not yet been possible to question her. Her condition is satisfactory.

She answers the following description: height, five feet five inches; fair complexion, light brown hair. Her pale green suit and darker green suède shoes bear the label of a Fifth Avenue store in New York. No handbag was found on the spot.

THE WAITRESS had had to leave the counter to serve an elderly couple who had just arrived in an open Cadillac. The man, who looked about seventy, stood tall and straight. His skin was tanned; he wore a white flannel suit and a pale blue tie, and his hair was the same silky white as that of his wife. Calm and smiling, they behaved as graciously in the cafeteria as they might have done in a drawing room, showing an extreme courtesy toward the waitress and exchanging small attentions between themselves. One could imagine them in a white mansion surrounded by immaculate lawns, which they had just left to visit their grandchildren; and surely the parcels on the red leather seat of the car must contain toys. After thirty or thirty-five years of living together they still delighted in one another, still outdid each other in attentiveness.

Steve, with the newspaper on his knees, did not realize that he was taking in every detail as he waited for the waitress, who was taking down their order, to come back to him. He had nothing special to say to her. He had nothing to say to anyone except Nancy. All he needed was for someone to pay him a little attention, even if it was only a friendly glance; and his pretext for waiting for the girl to come back was that he needed more change for the telephone.

When she had put the bacon on the hot-plate he murmured:

"It's my wife."

"I guessed it."

"Could you give me some more change?"

He handed her two dollars, and she picked some ten cent pieces.

"Drink your coffee first. Would you like a hot one?"

"Thanks."

He drank it to please her, almost out of gratitude, and went back to the call box and shut himself in.

The switchboard operator did not know yet, and exclaimed as she recognized his voice:

"You again? You'll go broke!"

"Get me the Waterly Hospital, in Rhode Island."

"Is someone sick?"

"My wife."

"I'm sorry."

"That's all right."

He heard her say:

"Providence? Give me the Waterly Hospital, and hurry up, honey. It's very urgent."

While she was waiting she spoke to him again.

"Did she have an accident? Was she the one you were expecting to find in Maine?"

"Yes."

"Waterly Hospital? One moment please."

He had not prepared anything to say. It was all new to him and he was awkward.

"I'd like to speak to Mrs. Hogan, miss. Mrs. Nancy Hogan."

He spelled the name. She repeated it to someone else, adding:

"Do you know that name? I don't see it on the list."

"Try the maternity floor."

He cut in:

"No, miss. My wife was injured on the highway last night, and taken to your hospital."

"One moment. There must be some mistake."

He could not understand why it should be so difficult to contact Nancy now that he had found her again.

"There's certainly a mistake," the voice confirmed after an interval. "The hospital has been full since eleven o'clock last night, and hasn't been able to accept any more patients. We even have beds in the corridors."

"The paper said——"

"Wait a minute. She may have been given first-aid in the emergency room and then transferred somewhere else. A week-end like this we do the best we can."

At the other end of the line, probably in the hospital yard, he heard an ambulance siren.

"I'd advise you to try New London. That's where we generally send——"

A man's voice called to the girl, who did not finish her sentence. Sure that the operator was listening, Steve said:

"Did you hear that?"

"Yes. They're rushed off their feet. Shall I get you New London?"

"Please. Will it take long?"

"I don't think so. Will you deposit forty cents please?"

He was suddenly so tired that if he had dared he would have asked the waitress to get the numbers for him. He had seen ambulances passing the night before, casualties waiting for first-aid at the side of the road, and he hadn't thought of the relatives who, like himself, had come up against silly difficulties in trying to find out what had happened.

"New London Hospital."

He repeated his little speech, spelled the name twice.

"You don't know if she's in Surgery?"

"I can't tell you. It's my wife. She was attacked on the highway."

He suddenly realized his own stupidity. Nancy couldn't be registered under her name since, according to the paper, she had not yet been identified.

"Wait a minute! Her name isn't on your list."

"What name is she registered under?"

"None. I've only just found out from the paper what happened to her."

"How old is she?"

"Thirty-four, but she looks thirty. The paper said thirty."

He would have to call Waterly again. They had looked for her under Hogan. True enough, they had said they had taken in no patients since eleven o'clock last night, but the receptionist might be mistaken.

"I'm sorry. We have no one answering that description. Several ambulances had to be directed on to other hospitals last night."

He waited to get the operator again.

"I want Waterly again."

She seemed embarrassed at reminding him of the money that must be deposited. He took a sip out of his bottle. Neither for pleasure nor from vice. His head was beginning to spin in the airless booth, of which he kept the door shut being loath to bother other people with his troubles.

The elderly couple were eating slowly, talking all the while, and he wondered what they found to say to one another after so long.

"I'm sorry to trouble you again, miss, but I've just realized my wife couldn't be registered under her name."

He explained the situation, laboriously making every detail clear. Beads stood out on his forehead. His shirt smelled of sweat. Was he going to Nancy in this condition, without even shaving?

"No, sir. I've checked thoroughly. Have you tried New London?"

He hung up in despair. It was the waitress who after hearing the result suggested:

"Why don't you try the police?"

He had four dollar bills left. The garage would have to accept a check. In the circumstances they could scarcely refuse.

"I need some more change. Sorry to bother you."

He felt humbled, walked to the box with rounded shoulders, his head bowed.

"Pennichuck Police?"

The resounding voice that answered seemed to fill the box.

"What do you want?"

He explained again. How many times had he done so?

"Sorry. It isn't for us. There's no one here but me. I heard about something like that, but it happened outside our area. Try the sheriff or the state police. I guess the state police would be better. They were patrolling all night. Better call Limestone 337."

Ever since he had contacted the police he had been haunted by the profile of Sid Halligan, a cigarette hanging from his lower lip.

"Yes. Yes. I heard something about it. The lieutenant who

investigated isn't here. He'll be back in an hour. What?... You're the husband?... Well, give me your name, I'll make a note. *H* for Harry, *O* for Oscar... O.K.... Were you there?... No? You don't know anything?... I suppose she was taken to Waterly Hospital... She isn't there?... You're sure?... Have you tried Lakefield? There was so much work last night that we put people wherever there was room..."

After Lakefield, where they knew nothing, he very nearly gave up, then decided to make one last attempt. Another hospital had been suggested to him, at Hayward, almost in the same district.

He scarcely dared to say his piece again, which was beginning to sound meaningless to him.

"Was a young woman brought in to you last night after being attacked on the highway?"

"Who is speaking, please?"

"Her husband. I've just seen the morning paper, and I'm sure it's my wife."

"Where are you?"

"In New Hampshire. Is she there?"

"If it's the patient with a head injury, yes."

"May I speak to her?"

"I'm sorry; there are no telephones except in the private rooms."

"I suppose she isn't well enough to come to the phone?"

"One moment. I'll ask the floor nurse. I don't think so."

He had found her at last! There were about a hundred and twenty miles between them, but at least he knew where she was. If she were dead, they would have told him already. At least the receptionist would have sounded embarrassed. What disappointed him was to learn that she was not in a private room. He pictured six or seven beds along a wall, the patients groaning with pain.

"Hello, are you still there?"

"Yes."

"Your wife can't come to the phone, and the doctor has left orders that she's not to be disturbed."

"How is she?"

"All right, I suppose."

"Has she recovered consciousness?"

"If you'll hold on a minute I'll put you through to the head nurse, who wants to speak to you."

The next voice, sharper than the receptionist's, was that of an older woman.

"I understand you're the husband of the injured woman?"

"Yes, Nurse. How is she?"

"As well as can be expected. The doctor examined her an hour ago and confirmed that the skull isn't fractured."

"Is she seriously hurt?"

"She's suffering mostly from shock."

"Has she recovered consciousness?"

There was a pause, a hesitation.

"The doctor wants her to rest, and he isn't allowing her to be questioned. Before leaving he gave her a sedative which should keep her asleep for some hours. Will you please give me your name?"

Was this the last time he'd have to spell it that day?

"And what about your address and telephone number?... The police were here first thing this morning, and they asked us to take down full particulars if anyone came to identify her. The lieutenant will come in again sometime today."

"I'm leaving right away. If my wife should wake, would you tell her that..."

Tell her what? That he was coming. There was nothing else to say.

"...I expect to be there in three or four hours. I don't know exactly when. I haven't looked at the map."

He added in an almost supplicating voice:

"I suppose you couldn't put her in a private room? Naturally I'll pay whatever——"

"My dear Mr. Hogan, you can think yourself lucky we've been able to find her a bed!"

Suddenly there were tears on his cheeks, for no reason, and he said with an uncalled-for fervor:

"Thank you so very much indeed, Nurse. Take good care of her!"

When he got back to the counter, the waitress, without a word, put a plate of bacon and eggs in front of him. He looked at her, surprised and uncertain.

"You must have something to eat."

"She's at Hayward."

"I know. I heard."

He had not realized he had been talking so loud. Other people had also heard and were gazing at him with a sympathetic interest.

"I'm wondering whether I should go and get the children first."

He started to eat, surprised at finding the fork in his hand.

"No. That would take at least three hours, and I don't want to take them to the hospital, I wouldn't know what to do with them."

He had to have some money; he hadn't enough left to pay for his breakfast, and there would be gasoline as well.

"Is it all right if I come back and pay you in a few minutes? I'll have to cash a check at the garage where I left my car."

He felt as though he were cheating. Everyone was nice to him because his wife had been attacked at the roadside and was now in the hospital; they spoke kindly to him, and thanks to Nancy's accident he no longer had any hesitation in offering a check. The garage proprietor, in the office where the tires were stacked, listened with increasing interest to his story.

"I absolutely must get to Hayward. I've lost my wallet and I have no papers with me, but you'll find my name and address in the car."

"How much money do you need?"

"I don't know. Twenty dollars? Forty?"

"You'd better take a spare wheel and a new tire."

"How long would that take?"

"Ten minutes. Where did you say your children were?"

"At Walla Walla Camp, in Maine, in charge of Mr. and Mrs. Keane."

"Why don't you call them up?"

He nearly said no, then realized that the garage proprietor had found this way of checking his identity, and he went at once into the call box, leaving the door open.

"Why, you've changed phones!" said the operator in surprise.

This time it was the husband who answered at the camp.

"This is Steve Hogan."

He had to listen to all the old boy scout wanted to tell him, waiting for a chance to get a word in.

"Mr. Keane, I wanted to tell you... My wife has had an accident on the highway. I've found out where she is, and I'm leaving right away for Hayward... No! I don't want to talk to the children just now. Don't tell them anything. Only that we'll be coming for them in a day or two. It won't be too inconvenient for you?... What?... I don't know. I don't know anything yet, Mr. Keane... Just don't let them suspect their mother's been hurt..."

As he finished talking the garage proprietor had taken some notes from a drawer, and had counted them out onto his desk.

"Make it out for forty dollars," he said.

He watched him closely as he signed the check and Steve wondered with discomfort whether he still had doubts as to his honesty. Only when he was at the door did the garageman lay a hand on his shoulder.

"You can count on me. Your car will be ready in ten minutes."

His hand was still on Steve's shoulder, the fingers hard as tools.

"Weren't you traveling with your wife last night?"

To avoid a lengthy explanation, Steve said no.

"My mechanic was puzzled when he found some women's clothes mixed up with the tools."

So ever since they had opened the trunk they had been watching him suspiciously. What had they thought? What had they supposed he had done? If the police had happened to call in, would they have said something?

"They belong to my wife," he muttered, not knowing what else to say.

Cars were becoming increasingly numerous on the road, and some of them were from New York. It was the second wave, people who didn't like traveling at night and started first thing on Saturday morning. There was yet a third wave to follow, with all the shop people, who had to work that morning and whose weekend did not begin until midday Saturday. *Forty-five million motorists...*

The waitress who had taken him under her wing said the wrong thing when he said good-by.

"Don't drive too fast. Be careful," she admonished him. "And drop in with your wife to say hello when you come back this way with the children."

So that, because of her warning, because of the state of exhaustion he was in, the highway, with its throbbing sound of thousands of tires speeding over the tarmac, frightened him. He got in behind the wheel, and had to wait some time before a gap enabled him to turn into the stream of cars heading toward Boston.

The seat beside him was empty. Generally it was Nancy's place. He seldom drove without having her there. Unlike the elderly couple in the Cadillac, they didn't talk much. He recalled the movement of his wife's arm as she reached out and switched on the radio after they had gone a few miles. On Sundays, in the spring and autumn, when they went out for a drive, the children would be in the back, often not sitting back, but preferring to lean their elbows on the rear of the front seat. His daughter would be just behind him, and he felt her breath on his neck. She talked incessantly about anything and everything, about the passing cars and about the countryside, assertive and self-assured, shrugging her shoulders condescendingly when her brother volunteered an opinion.

"Hurry up, camp time!" Nancy and he were apt to sigh when they returned, worn out, from one of these expeditions.

And then when summer came they didn't take advantage of their freedom.

It seemed so strange to be alone that he had a feeling of shame. Glancing at the empty seat, he thought of Halligan, who had occupied it for part of the night, and once again his fingers began to twitch with impatience. He needed a mouthful of whiskey if he was to drive even passably well. His very safety required it. He was so feverish that he was continually afraid of jerking the wheel and colliding with the cars in the next lane.

He waited until no one could see, and then put the bottle to his lips. Even Nancy would have understood and approved. The morning after the night when she had had to undress him and put him to bed, she had herself brought a glass of whiskey into the bathroom where he had stood looking more like a ghost than a man.

"You'll feel a little more solid with this inside you."

He swore to himself that he wouldn't go into a bar whatever happened, or stop to buy another bottle.

Despite his impatience, he did not let the speedometer exceed fifty, and he stopped as soon as the lights turned yellow.

He had feared losing his way in Boston, where Nancy generally directed him, but he passed through the city as though by a miracle and found himself on the right road, over which he had traveled the night before without knowing it.

There was no way of avoiding Providence. He was surprised to find it a bright and pleasant town. Past it he wouldn't have to follow last night's route, passing the bars where he had stopped, since he was to turn off at once toward the entrance to the bay.

Would this police lieutenant of whom the nurse had spoken want to question him? Would he be asked to account for his actions during the night? He would certainly have to explain why he had not been with his wife at the moment she was attacked. The simplest thing would be to tell the truth, at least in part, and admit that they had quarreled. Was there a married couple anywhere that did not have a quarrel of that kind? Were there many men who never drank a drop too much?

The most remarkable thing was that at the time Nancy left the car he hadn't been drunk. He may have been "in the tunnel," to use his own expression, and he had had just enough to drink to make him short-tempered with Nancy, but if she hadn't gone off probably nothing would have happened. They would have bickered for the rest of the way. He would have complained that she did not treat him like a man, and perhaps, as usual on these occasions, he would have accused her of preferring the offices of Schwartz & Taylor to their own home.

It was unfair. If she had not gone back to work after the children were born, they would not have been able to buy that house, even on twelve-year terms. Neither would they have had a car. They would have been forced to live in the inner suburbs, because they could not have gone on indefinitely living in a three-room apartment as they had done at the beginning.

All this she pointed out to him in a calm voice, a little more flat than usual, her nostrils slightly pinched as happened only when she said something disagreeable.

But it was still true that she was happy in her office, where she was a person of consequence, treated with respect. For instance, when Steve telephoned her, the girl on the switchboard invariably answered:

"One moment, Mr. Hogan. I'll see if Mrs. Hogan's free."

And sometimes after handling the plugs:

"Could you call again a little later? Mrs. Hogan's in conference."

With Mr. Schwartz undoubtedly. Perhaps he never did make a pass at her. His wife was one of the prettiest women in New York, a former model whose name kept cropping up in the gossip columns. Despite the exaggerated attention Schwartz paid to his appearance, Steve, who had met him a number of times, thought him repulsive.

He was quite certain there was nothing between them. Yet it still stung like a slap in the face whenever Nancy said:

"Max was talking to me today about..."

Had she and Steve been discussing the theater she would cut him short with:

"It isn't worth seeing. Max went last night."

Was he going to start on his grievances again? Had he forgotten already that Nancy was lying injured in a hospital bed? He had not dared ask the nurse on what part of the head she had been hit, or whether she was disfigured.

To try and stop himself thinking, he switched on the radio, did not listen to it, and took some time to reflect that it was perhaps indecent to be listening to songs on his way to his wife's bedside. It hurt him to have left the children at the camp. He did not know when he would be able to get them. The Keanes closed the camp during the winter, which they spent in Florida. They were reputed to be very rich, and perhaps it was true.

The first signboard indicating Hayward made him feverish again. He had only another fifteen miles to go, on a road congested with cars heading for the ferry to take them over to some islands. He took advantage of a pause in the traffic to bend low under cover of the dashboard and finish his bottle, which he threw in the ditch.

It would be time enough later on to think about shaving and buying clean clothes. A clock said twelve as he reached the town, and it took him a little while to get out of the procession of cars pushing him toward the ferry.

"How do I get to the hospital, please?"

Someone told him, but he had to ask again. It was a red-brick building with three stories of windows behind which beds could be seen. Five cars parked in the front courtyard bore doctors' license plates and a stretcher was being carefully lowered from an ambulance.

He found the patients' and visitors' entrance, and went to the reception window.

"Steve Hogan," he said. "I'm the one who called a little while ago from New Hampshire about my wife."

There were two of them, dressed in white, and one glanced curiously at him as she telephoned. The other, plump and red-headed, murmured:

"I don't think you'll be able to go up. Visiting hours are at two and seven."

"But..."

Must they really stick to visiting hours in a case like his?

"The head nurse told me——"

"Just a moment. Please have a seat."

There were six people seated in the entrance hall, among them two little colored boys who wore their best suits and never moved. No one paid any attention to him. He could hear the voices in the reception office. They were ringing all the floors for a doctor whose name he could not catch, and when they got him they asked him to come to Emergency right away, no doubt for the patient who had just been brought in by ambulance.

Everything was as white and bright and clean as in the cafeteria, with sun streaming in through the bay windows, and flowers in a corner, perhaps ten bunches and baskets, waiting to be taken up to the rooms.

The two little colored boys, sitting with their caps on their knees, had the same expression they must wear in church. A middle-aged woman, near them, stared fixedly out of the window; a man was reading a magazine as absorbedly as though he had hours to wait, and another lit a cigarette, glanced at the watch on his wrist.

Steve was surprised to find himself more collected than he had been a quarter of an hour earlier in the car. Everyone around him was calm. An old man in white hospital garb, his twisted body huddled in a rubber-tired wheel chair, which he propelled with thin hands, traveled the entire length of the corridor to come and look at them. His lower lip hung and his expression was at once childish and cunning. After carefully examining each one, he turned the chair around and went back to his room.

Was it about Steve they were now talking over the phone? Steve did not dare ask, guessing that in this place nothing he said could serve any purpose.

"Will you come down? No? Shall I send him up?"

The one who was speaking gave him a quick glance through the window and said in reply to a question:

"It's hard to tell... So-so..."

In what way was he "so-so"? Did she mean that he did not seem to be too agitated and might be allowed to go up?

The girl put down the receiver and beckoned to him.

"If you will go up to the first floor, the head nurse will see you."

"Thank you."

"Turn to your right at the end of the corridor and wait for the elevator."

All the way along he saw open doorways, men and women lying or sitting up in bed, some sitting in armchairs, others with a leg in plaster that was held up by a pulley.

No one seemed to be in pain, or showed any annoyance or impatience. He nearly bumped into a young woman who wore nothing but a coarse cotton nightdress and was coming out of the toilet.

He spoke to a passing nurse:

"Excuse me, miss—the elevator, please."

"The second door. It'll be down in a minute."

Indeed, a light on the wall, which he hadn't noticed, shone red. A doctor in a white smock, with a cap on his head and a white mask hanging down on his chest, also gave Steve a sharp look as he passed.

"First floor."

The old, white-headed elevator operator seemed even more unconcerned than the rest of them, and the more deeply Steve penetrated into the hospital, the more he lost his personality, the ability to think and feel. He was very near Nancy, under the same roof. In a few moments, perhaps, he would see her, and yet he scarcely thought of her. Emptiness had insensibly taken hold of him, and he mechanically followed whatever instructions he might be given.

The corridors on the first floor formed a cross in the middle of which stood a long desk. A grayhaired sister in glasses was seated with a register in front of her. There was a notice board on the wall opposite, and near the register a rack of phials plugged with cotton wool.

"Mr. Hogan?" she asked, having kept him standing there for at least a minute before she looked up from her papers.

"Yes, Nurse. How is . . . ?"

"Please sit down."

She got up and went along one of the corridors, and for a moment he thought she was going to get Nancy. But she had gone to see another patient, and presently she came back with a phial bearing a label, which she put in a rack.

"Your wife hasn't awakened yet. She'll probably go on sleeping for some time."

Why did he feel obliged to nod and smile with an appearance of gratitude?

"You can wait downstairs if you like, and I'll send for you when you can see her?"

"Has she been in much pain?"

"I don't think so. She received treatment as soon as she was found. She seems to have a sound constitution."

"She's never been really ill."

"She has had children, hasn't she?"

The question surprised him, and the way she asked it; but he answered like a child in school:

"Two."

"Recently?"

"Our daughter is ten and the boy eight."

"No miscarriage?"

"No."

He dared not utter a word on his own account. In any case, what question would he have asked?

"You spent the day with her yesterday?"

"Not the day. We work in separate jobs in New York."

"But you saw her in the evening?"

"We traveled part of the way together."

"When you see her you mustn't forget that she has had a very severe shock. She will still be under the influence of sedatives. You mustn't get excited or say anything that might upset her."

"I promise. Has she . . . ?"

"Has she what?"

"I wanted to ask if she had recovered consciousness."

"Partly, on two occasions."

"Did she say anything?"

"Not yet. I thought I'd told you over the phone."

"I'm sorry."

"You must go down now. I've called up Lieutenant Murray to tell him you're here. He'll certainly want to see you."

She rose and he was obliged to do the same.

"You can go by the stairs. This way."

As on the ground floor, all the doors were open, including the one to the ward where Nancy was, no doubt. He would have liked to ask permission to see her for a second, even to look at her bed from the doorway.

He did not try to. He pushed open the glass-paned door he had been shown and found himself on a stairway that a janitress was busy cleaning. Down below he got lost again, but ended by finding his way back to the entrance hall, from which the two little colored boys had departed.

He went to the reception window and said:

"I've been told to wait here."

"That's right. The lieutenant will be here in a few minutes."

He sat down. He was the only one in the place who wore a soiled and crumpled shirt and was unshaven. He wished now that he had cleaned up before coming to the hospital, where he was no longer master of his own actions. He could have bought shaving things and a toothbrush and gone into one of the streetcar depots, for example, where there were washing facilities for travelers.

What was Lieutenant Murray going to think of him, seeing the state he was in?

However, he plucked up courage to light a cigarette, since someone else was smoking, and then went and had a drink at the water fountain. He was trying to foresee the questions that would be put to him and to think of suitable replies, but his mind was still cloudy, and, like the woman near him, he gazed fixedly through the open window at a tree outlined against the blue sky, its immobility, in the still, midday air, giving an impression of eternity.

It cost him an effort to remain fully aware of what he was doing here, of what had happened since last night, and even of his own identity. Was it really true that he possessed two children, one of them a fast-growing daughter, in a camp in Maine, and a fifteen-thousand-dollar house on Long Island; and that on Tuesday morning—in two days' time!—he would take his place behind the inquiry desk at World Travelers, to spend hours answering the customers' questions and operating two or three telephones?

From here, it all seemed improbable, ludicrous, and, as though to enhance the feeling of unreality, a steamship's siren rent the silence, close at hand, and, looking through the other window, he saw a black funnel ringed with red rising above the roofs, and he could clearly see the little white jet of steam.

A ship was setting off over the same sea that he had contemplated that morning through the New Hampshire pines, the sea at the edge of which Bonnie and Dan played at this very moment, wondering why their father and mother did not come for them.

The head nurse had not seemed worried about Nancy's condition. Would she have been worried even if Nancy had been at death's door? How many people died every week in that hospital? Did they talk about it? Did the word go around:

"The woman in No. 7 died last night"?

They must be taken out by some other door, and the patients must not know. The old man in the wheel chair came around to see if there were any new faces, seemed disappointed at not finding any.

A car pulled up on the gravel drive. Steve did not rise to go and look. He did not have the strength. He was sleepy and his eyelids were pricking. He heard footsteps, felt sure they came for him, remained seated.

A lieutenant in the uniform of the state police, his high boots shining, his cheeks as smoothly shaved and tanned as those of the old gentleman in the Cadillac, came in briskly and went to the reception window, behind which the girl merely pointed to Steve.

6

HE HADN'T noticed when he'd gone up to see the sister that the first doorway on the left of the corridor was inscribed, "Director." The door was open like the others, and a bald-headed man in shirt sleeves sat at a desk working. The lieutenant called to him familiarly:

"O.K. if I use the conference room for a little while?"

The director recognized his voice and nodded without looking round. It was the room next door, bathed in golden half-light from the thin bars of sunshine that filtered between the slats of the drawn venetian blinds. On the pastel walls hung photographs of venerable and solemn gentlemen, no doubt the founders of the hospital. A long table, so highly polished that it clearly reflected one's face, occupied the center of the room, surrounded by ten chairs with seats of light-colored leather.

The door of this room, too, was left open onto the corridor along which a nurse or a patient passed from time to time. The lieutenant sat down at the end of the table, his back to the window, got a notebook out of his pocket, opened it at a blank page, and adjusted his mechanical pencil.

"Sit down."

In the entrance hall, he had scarcely looked at Steve, merely signing to him to follow; nor did he show any more interest in him now. He wrote a few words in a small hand at the head of the page, glanced at his wrist to see the time, and wrote this down too, as though it were a matter of importance.

He was a man of about forty, athletic in build, with a slight tendency to stoutness. When he pulled off his stiff-peaked cap and laid it on the table, Steve thought he looked younger and less awe-inspiring, because of his short, reddish-blond hair, as curly as lamb's wool.

"Hogan, isn't it?"

"Yes. Stephen Walter Hogan. Everybody calls me Steve."

"Place of birth?"

"Groveton, Vermont. My father was an agent for chemical products."

It was silly to add this. It was because, whenever he said he came from Vermont, people always said,

"A farmer, eh?"

Actually, his father wasn't a farmer, nor his grandfather, who had been lieutenant governor. It was Nancy's father who was a farmer in Kansas, and was descended from Irish immigrants.

"Address?" asked the lieutenant in an impersonal voice, his head still bent over his notebook.

"Scottville, Long Island."

The window was open and a slight breeze stirred in the room where the two men occupied only a tiny part of the huge table around which eight chairs remained vacant. Despite the coolness of this draft Steve would have preferred to have the door shut, but it was not for him to suggest it. His attention was distracted by the coming and going of people along the corridor.

"Age?"

"Thirty-two. Thirty-three in December."

"Occupation?"

"I work for World Travelers on Madison Avenue."

"Since when?"

"Twelve years."

He could not see the sense of putting all this down in the notebook.

"You started there at nineteen?"

"Yes. Right after my second year in college."

"I suppose you're sure it's your wife who's been injured? Have you seen her?"

"They haven't let me see her yet. But I'm sure it's her."

"Because of the description of her and her clothes published in the papers?"

"And also the place where it happened."

"You were there?"

This time he looked up, but the glance he gave Steve, as though unintentional, by accident, remained indifferent. Steve blushed nonetheless, hesitated, gulped before saying:

"The fact is, I had left the car for a few minutes, outside a bar and——"

The other cut him short.

"I think we'd better begin at the beginning. How long have you been married?"

"Eleven years."

"How old is your wife?"

"Thirty-four."

"Does she work too?"

"She works for the firm of Schwartz & Taylor, 625 Fifth Avenue."

He took pains to answer precisely, gradually dismissing the idea that these questions were of no importance. The lieutenant was not much older than himself. He wore a wedding ring, probably had children. For all Steve knew, they probably had about the same income, the same kind of house and family life. Why didn't he feel more at ease with him? For the past few minutes he was afflicted with the shyness he had felt as a schoolboy in front of his teachers, the same as he'd felt for a long time in front of his boss and had never lost in the presence of Mr. Schwartz.

"Any children?"

"Two, a boy and a girl."

He did not wait for the next question.

"The girl is ten and the boy's eight. They both spent the summer at Walla Walla Camp, in Maine, with Mr. and Mrs. Keane, and we were driving up for them yesterday evening."

He would have appreciated a smile, a sign of encouragement. The lieutenant merely wrote away and Steve could not tell what was being written, had tried in vain to read it upside down. There was nothing surly in the officer's manner, nothing harsh or threatening. Very likely he, too, was tired after having spent the night on patrol and not having been to bed. At least he had been able to have a bath and a shave!

"What time did you leave New York?"

"A little after five—say twenty-past, at the latest."

"Did you pick up your wife at her office?"

"We met as usual in a bar on Forty-fifth Street."

"What did you drink?"

"A martini. Then we went home to get a bite to eat and collect our things."

"Did you have anything more to drink?"

"No."

He hesitated to lie. He had to remind himself, to ease his conscience, that he was not testifying under oath. He did not understand why he was being questioned in so much detail when he was here simply to identify his wife, who had been attacked on the road.

It increased his discomfort to see the old man in the wheel chair loom in the doorway, and stare at him, his hanging lip and his paralyzed face making him seem to be sneering silently.

The lieutenant paid no attention.

"You probably took clothes to last you a couple of days. Is that what you call your things?"

"Yes."

Their interview scarcely begun, an apparently simple question already put him in an awkward position.

"What time did you leave Long Island?"

"Around seven or seven-thirty. We had to drive very slowly at first because of the heavy traffic."

"How do you get on with your wife?"

"We get on very well."

He had not dared answer, because of the notebook, where he could see his replies being entered:

"We love each other."

Yet it was the truth.

"Where was your first stop?"

He did not even attempt to hedge.

"I don't know exactly. It was immediately after we left the Merritt Parkway. I don't remember the name of the place."

"Did your wife go with you?"

"She stayed in the car."

Apart from Sid Halligan he had nothing to hide, and what had happened with Sid had nothing to do with his wife, since he had met him long after the attack.

"What did you have to drink?"

"A rye."

"Is that all?"

"Yes."

"A double?"

"Yes."

"When did you start quarreling?"

"We didn't exactly quarrel. I knew Nancy was annoyed that I'd stopped for a drink."

Everything around them was so calm and silent that they seemed to be living in an unreal world where nothing mattered any more except the doings of one Steve Hogan. The conference room, with its long table, became a strange place of judgment where there was no judge, no prosecutor, only an official writing down his words, and on the walls seven gentlemen, long dead, who represented eternity.

He felt no resentment. Not for an instant was he tempted to stand up and say that all this was nobody's business but his own, that he was in a free country and that it would be for him to call the police to account for having allowed an unknown ruffian to attack his wife by the roadside.

On the contrary, he tried to explain.

"At those times I'm apt to get short-tempered too, and I tend to be cross with her. I suppose it's the same in every family."

Murray did not smile, or agree, kept on writing, indifferently, as though it were not for him to express an opinion.

A nurse whom Steve had not seen before stopped in the doorway and knocked on the woodwork to attract attention.

"Will you be coming soon to see the accident case, Lieutenant?"

"How is he?"

"They're giving him a transfusion. He has regained consciousness and says he can describe the car that knocked him down."

"Ask the sergeant, who's in my car, to take down his statement and do whatever's necessary. I'll see him later."

He continued his set of questions.

"In that bar where you stopped..."

"Which one?"

He had spoken too quickly, but that shouldn't matter much, because they would have to come to it sooner or later.

"The first one. You didn't happen to strike up an acquaintance with anyone next to you at the bar?"

"Not in that one, no."

He was ashamed already of what was bound to follow. All his actions, which seemed so commonplace and innocent the night before, when there were one or two million Americans having drinks along the highways, now assumed a different aspect, even in his own eyes; and he rubbed his hand over his cheeks as though the beard that roughened them bore witness to his guilt.

"Your wife threatened to leave?"

He did not immediately grasp the implication of that question. Did the lieutenant realize that he hadn't been to bed, and that he was reaching a state of weariness that made it a great effort to understand the meaning of words?

"Only when I wanted to stop the second time," he said.

"She had already threatened to do so before?"

"I don't remember."

"Did she talk about a divorce?"

He looked at his questioner in sudden anger, frowned, and banged his fist on the table.

"But there was never any question of that! What are you driving at? I had a drink too many. I wanted another. We had a more or less bitter argument. My wife warned me that if I got out of the car again to go in a bar she'd drive on without me...."

His anger was turning slowly into a painful stupefaction.

"You really thought she meant to leave me for good? But..."

The thought opened up such horizons that there were no words to express what he felt. It was worse than all he had imagined. If the lieutenant was so meticulously noting his replies, keeping an expressionless face, showing him none of the consideration one feels for any husband whose wife has been seriously injured, it was because he thought he was the one who...

He forgot all about the open door and raised his voice, though not in indignation, because he was too crushed with amazement to feel indignant any more:

"You really thought that! But Lieutenant, look at me, for God's sake, look me straight in the face, and tell me if I look like..."

He did look precisely like a man who might have done anything, including what he had in mind, what with his watery eyes, his puffed lids, his two-day beard, and his dirty shirt. His breath reeked of whiskey and his hands, as soon as they no longer clung to the table, began to shake.

"Ask Nancy! She'll tell you that never——"

He had to break off to repeat, because it choked him:

"You thought that!"

After which he slumped back on his chair, resigned, without the energy or the wish to defend himself. Let them do what they liked with him! In a little while, anyway, Nancy would tell them....

And now another thought occurred to him, a hideous thought that kept growing, that engulfed all others. What if Nancy should not recover consciousness?

Almost haggardly, he stared at the lieutenant, who twisted the end of his mechanical pencil and said evenly:

"For reasons you'll learn later, we know, since ten o'clock this morning, that you didn't assault your wife."

"And until ten?"

"It's our job to examine all the possibilities without rejecting any out of hand. Take it easy, Mr. Hogan. I never intended to frighten you with tricky questions. You're the one who's jumping to conclusions. But it could very well have happened, if quarrels like the one you had last night had been frequent enough, that your wife should think about a divorce. That's all I meant."

"It doesn't happen to us once a year. I'm not a drunkard, not even what you'd call a steady drinker. I..."

This time, because a child had stopped in the doorway and was listening to them, the lieutenant went to shut the door. When he came back, Steve, who had been thinking about what could have taken place at ten o'clock that morning, asked:

"You've arrested the man who did it?"

"We'll come to that in a little while. Why, when you stopped in front of the second bar, didn't your wife drive on as she had threatened to?"

"Because I put the ignition key in my pocket."

Would it become clear at last that it was all quite simple?

"I thought I'd teach her a lesson; I was sure she deserved one, because she's often too sure of herself. After two drinks, especially rye, which doesn't suit me, things look different."

He argued the point without conviction, no longer believing in what he said. What else would they ask him about? He had supposed that the only embarrassing topic concerned Halligan, but so far he hadn't been mentioned.

"Do you know what time it was when you got out of the car?"

"No. The clock on the dashboard hasn't been going for a long time."

"Your wife didn't say that she'd go on just the same?"

He had to make an effort. He no longer knew where he was.

"No. I don't think so."

"You aren't sure?"

"No. Wait a minute. It seems to me that if she'd said anything about the bus I'd have known she meant it and would have stopped her. I'm sure of that, now! I didn't think of the bus until afterwards, when I saw the lights at the crossroad. And another thing! I remember that when I didn't find her in the car I started calling her in the dark in the parking lot."

He didn't remember about the message Nancy had left on the seat.

"Did you notice the other cars?"

"Just a minute."

He wanted to seem co-operative, to help the police as best he could.

"I thought they were mostly jalopies and trucks. Now maybe it wasn't at that same bar."

"Was it called Armando's?"

"It could be. The name seems to ring a bell."

"Would you recognize it again?"

"Probably. There was a television set to the right of the bar."

He preferred not to mention the little girl in the closet with the bar of chocolate.

"Go on."

"There were a lot of people, men and women. I remember a couple who never moved and didn't speak."

"You didn't notice anyone in particular?"

". . . No."

"Did you speak to anyone?"

"A man next to me offered me a drink. I was going to refuse when the bartender motioned me to take it, probably because the guy, who was a little high, would have insisted and perhaps started a row. You know how those things go."

"Did he have one on you too?"

"I guess so. Yes. Probably."

"You talked to him about your wife?"

"Maybe so. More likely about women in general."

"You didn't tell him about the key?"

He was worn out. He didn't know any more. With the best will in the world he was beginning to mix everything up, confusing his conversation with the fair-haired man with blue eyes and the things he had said to Halligan. Even the two bars were running together in his memory. His head ached, the back of his eyes ached. His shirt was sticking to his body and he was aware that he smelled unpleasant.

"You didn't notice if this man went out before you?"

"I'm sure he didn't. I went out first."

"You're absolutely sure?"

He would reach the point where he was no longer certain of anything.

"I could swear I left first. I remember paying and walking toward the door. I turned around. Yes, he was still there."

"And your wife, she was no longer in the car?"

"That's right."

There was a knock at the door. It was a police sergeant in uniform, who indicated to his chief that he had something to say to him. He allowed only one of his hands to appear, as though the other held something he did not want Steve to see.

The lieutenant rose to join him and they exchanged a few words in low voices outside the door. When Murray returned, alone, he threw a handful of clothes and undergarments on the table without saying anything—Nancy's things, which they had found in the trunk of the car.

They must have suspected him of something, since they had searched the car, parked in the hospital courtyard.

The lieutenant sat down again at the end of the table, avoiding any reference to what had just happened. He went on in the same impersonal voice:

"We'd got to where you came out of Armando's and found that your wife had disappeared."

"I called her, thinking for sure she'd got out to stretch her legs."

"Was it raining?"

"No... Yes..."

"You didn't see anyone near the parking lot?"

"Nobody."

"You left right away?"

"When I saw there was a crossroad not far off, and remembered Nancy's threat, I thought of the bus. We'd passed a Greyhound earlier in the evening. I guess that's what gave me the idea. I drove slowly, watching the right-hand side of the road, hoping I'd catch up with her."

"You didn't see her?"

"I didn't see anything."

"How long did you stay in Armando's?"

"I thought I stayed about ten minutes, a quarter of an hour at most."

"But it could have been longer?"

Steve smiled piteously at his inquisitor.

"The state I'm in . . ." he murmured bitterly.

He scarcely knew any longer that he had found Nancy, that she was a few steps away from him, that before long he would see her, speak to her, perhaps take her in his arms. Was he sure that they would allow him to?

The strange thing was that he bore them no grudge, that he had no resentment, that he felt genuinely guilty.

By a cruel irony, there came back to him now things he had said to Sid Halligan in a sodden voice. It had started with the railroad tracks, of course, the tracks and the highways, and he had gone on to talk about people who are afraid of life because they aren't true men.

"So, you see, they make rules that they call laws, and they call sin anything that scares them in other people. That's the truth, brother! If they didn't shake in their boots, if they were real men, they'd have no need for police forces and law courts, for preachers and churches, no need for banks, for life-insurance, for Sunday schools and red and green lights at the street corners. Does a guy like you give a damn for all that? But here you are, thumbing your nose at them! They're hundreds looking for you along the roads and bawling your name in every news bulletin, and so what do you do? You quietly drive on, smoking a cigarette, and you say 'nuts' to them!"

It had been longer, involved, and he remembered that he kept seeking his companion's approval, just a word, a sign, and that Halligan had seemed not to be listening. Perhaps he had snapped, once again, with the cigarette glued to his lower lip:

"Shut up!"

That morning it was Nancy's forgiveness he had resolved to ask. But it was not only to her that he owed atonement; it was a whole world, embodied in this police lieutenant with curly, ginger hair, that had rights over him.

"When I got to the crossroad I inquired at the cafeteria on the corner. The waitress at the counter can confirm it. First, I asked her if she'd seen my wife."

"I know."

"She told you?"

"Yes."

He had never imagined that his words and actions would one day assume so much importance.

"Did she also tell you that it was from her I found out that the bus had gone?"

"That's right. You got back in your car and, to use her own words, drove off like crazy."

This was the only time the lieutenant allowed a faint smile to break through.

"I planned to overtake the bus and persuade her to come with me."

"Did you catch it?"

"No."

"What speed were you driving at?"

"Sometimes over seventy. It's surprising I didn't get a speeding ticket."

"It's even more surprising you didn't have an accident."

"Yes," he admitted, hanging his head.

"How do you explain that, going at that speed, you weren't able to overtake a bus that wasn't going over fifty?"

"I got on the wrong road."

"Do you know where you went?"

"No. Once before, earlier in the evening when my wife was still with me, I'd taken the wrong road, but we had ended back on the highway. By myself, I just went round in circles."

"Without stopping anywhere?"

What was he going to do? The moment he had been fearing since he first opened his eyes, alone in the car at the edge of the pinewoods, had come. That morning, he had decided to say nothing, without knowing exactly why. Of course, it was humiliating to have to tell Nancy about his encounter with Halligan. But his decision had also been prompted by the wish to avoid a lengthy interrogation by the police.

And now, like it or not, he had been subjected to the interrogation for nearly an hour; he wondered how he had been caught in the web; he saw himself following the lieutenant into the room with the long table, sufficiently easy in his mind to study the photographs of the old gentlemen.

He had expected some formality. Right at the start he had said more than he had been asked. Now he was beginning to think of himself as a cornered animal. It was no longer a question of Nancy or of Halligan, but of himself, and he would have been scarcely surprised to be told that his life was at stake.

For thirty-two years, nearly thirty-three, he had been an honest man; he had followed the tracks, as he had proclaimed last night with so much vehemence, being a good son, good student, employee, husband, father, and the owner of a house on Long Island; he had never broken any law, never been summoned before any court and every Sunday morning he had gone to church with his family. He was a happy man. He lacked nothing.

Then where did they come from, all those things he said when he'd had a drink too many and started by attacking Nancy before assailing society as a whole? They had to spring from somewhere. The same phenomenon occurred each time, and each time his rebellion followed exactly the same course.

If he believed the things he said at those times, if they were a part of his personality, of his character, would he not continue to believe them next morning?

But the next day, his feeling was invariably one of shame, accompanied by a vague apprehension, as though he realized he had been unfaithful to someone or something, to Nancy first of all, whose forgiveness he always asked, but also to the community, to a more indefinable power that would have had a claim upon him.

This payment of accounts was now being demanded of him. He had not yet been accused. The lieutenant had not reproached him in any way, merely asking questions and noting down the replies, which seemed even more ominous, and he had tossed Nancy's belongings onto the table without once referring to them.

What deterred Steve from confessing everything without waiting to be compelled to do so?

This question he did not dare answer. Besides it was complicated. After what had happened between them, wouldn't it be a dirty trick, and cowardly, to give Halligan away?

More and more he was convinced that he had made himself his accomplice, and in law this was true. Not only had he not attempted to hinder his escape, but he had helped it, and not because of the revolver leveled at him.

It had to be remembered that at the time he was living his night!

In the morning he had telephoned hotels, hospitals, the police. Had he said a word about the fugitive from Sing Sing?

He had a few seconds left in which to choose. The lieutenant did not press him, waiting with remarkable patience.

What had the last question been?

"Without stopping anywhere? . . ."

"I stopped once more," he said.

"Do you know where?"

He stayed silent, staring at the golden reflections on the table, certain that the policeman was weighing his silence.

"At a log cabin."

The lieutenant repeated:

"Whereabouts?"

"Just outside Providence. There was a roadhouse next door."

Why did he feel a sudden break in the tension? How could the reply relieve the lieutenant, who now looked at him, not merely with the eyes of an official carrying out a routine assignment, but, it seemed to him, with the eyes of a man.

Steve was touched by it. This morning, too, people had looked at him that way, but then, to the waitress in the cafeteria and the telephone operator, he had been simply a man who has just received bad news. They knew nothing of the night he had spent. The garage proprietor was the only one who suspected anything.

Had the man with the cigar in fact passed his suspicions on to the police? It could be. Steve had offered no reasonable explanation about the trunk, which is an unlikely place for finding women's underwear mixed up with the tools. Nor had he explained how or where he had lost his wallet and papers.

Anything was possible, and he was now convinced that, long before they both sat down at the end of the long table where eight chairs remained empty, Lieutenant Murray already knew.

The lieutenant also seemed sensitive to the slightest changes and it took him only one look at Steve to know that he was ready to make a clean breast of it.

"Did he tell you his name?" he asked as though he were sure of being understood.

"I don't remember if he was the one. Wait a minute..."

He was smiling now, almost amused by his own perturbation.

"I've got everything so mixed up... I was the one... Yes, I'm almost certain I was the one who guessed when I found him in the car... They had just been talking about him on the radio...."

He was coming to the surface, taking a deep breath, and looked around in annoyance as someone knocked at the door.

"Come in!"

The sister from the first floor spoke, not to Steve, but to the policeman, whom she seemed to know well.

"The doctor says he can come up."

She went up to the lieutenant, leaned forward, and whispered something in his ear. The lieutenant shook his head and she said something else.

"Listen, Hogan," Lieutenant Murray said at last. "There are certain facts. I still haven't had a chance to tell you. It's partly your own fault. First, I had to find out..."

Steve nodded to show that he understood. If he had talked at once it would have been over long ago and now he found his own obstinacy absurd.

"Your wife is out of danger. The doctor's definite about that. But she's still in a state of shock. Whatever her attitude may be, whatever she may say, it's important that you should keep calm."

He did not quite understand what this meant, and, with a lump in his throat, he said obediently:

"I promise."

All he knew was that he was going to see her, and at the thought a shiver ran down his back. He followed the sister out into the corridor, while the lieutenant came behind, moving noiselessly in his boots.

They didn't take the elevator, but went up the stairway and came to the crossing formed by the corridors. He would have been incapable of saying, later, whether they turned to the right or to the left. They passed three open doorways, and he avoided looking in; a doctor came out of the fourth room, nodded to the sister that all was well, looked hard at Steve, and shook hands with the lieutenant.

"How are you, Bill?"

Those words became etched on his memory as though they had possessed the utmost importance. His legs felt weak. On his left, he saw three beds against the wall—not six as he had pictured them that morning—an old woman sitting up in her bed near the window, reading; another, with her hair hanging down in braids, seated in a chair; and a third who seemed to be asleep and was breathing with difficulty. None of them was Nancy. She was on the other side, where there were three more beds, in the one that had been hidden from him by the door.

When he saw her he spoke her name, at first in a whisper; then he repeated it more loudly, trying to make his voice sound cheerful for her sake, so that she shouldn't be frightened. He did not understand why she was looking at him with a sort of terror, so that the sister thought it necessary to go over and pat her shoulder, murmuring:

"He's here, you see? He's happy to have found you. Everything's going to be all right."

"Nancy!" he called, no longer able to hide his anguish.

He did not recognize the look in her eyes. The bandages that encircled her head down to the eyebrows and hid her ears perhaps changed the appearance of her face. It was so white that it seemed to be without life, and her lips, so pale, seemed different. He had never seen them so thin, so pinched, like the lips of an old woman. He had expected all this; he could, he should have been expecting it all, but he did not expect those eyes, which were afraid of him and abruptly turned away.

He came closer and held one of her hands lying on the sheet.

"Nancy, honey, forgive me..."

He had to bend down to catch her reply.

"Don't talk..." she said.

"Nancy, I'm here. You'll get well quickly, the doctor's sure of it. Everything's fine. We..."

Why would she still not look at him? Why did she turn her face to the wall?

"Tomorrow I'm driving up to camp for the children. They're fine too. You'll see them..."

"Steve!"

He thought she wanted him to bend still lower.

"Yes, I'm listening. I'm so glad I've found you! How I hated myself for being such a fool!"

"Ssh! . . ."

She wanted to speak, but first she had to get her breath.

"They told you?" she asked then, as he saw tears rolling down her cheeks and he clenched his teeth so that he could hear them grating.

The sister touched his arm as though to convey a message and he murmured:

"Why, sure. They told me."

"Can you ever forgive me?"

"But, Nancy, I'm the one that needs to be forgiven, I'm the one who——"

"Ssh . . ." she said again.

Slowly, she turned her face to look at him, but as he bent down to touch it with his lips, she pushed her arms against him weakly, crying:

"No! No! No! I can't!"

He straightened up in astonishment, and the doctor came into the ward and went to the head of the bed while the sister whispered:

"You must come now. It's better to leave her alone."

7

IT MIGHT have been happening on another planet.

The idea of asking any question did not occur to him, nor of making any decision, of taking the slightest initiative; he would scarcely have been surprised if someone had walked through him like a ghost.

With a hand on his shoulder the lieutenant guided him toward a window at the end of the corridor and they had to thrust their way through a torrent of people who, as though at a signal, had invaded the first floor, men, women, and children in their Sunday clothes, many carrying flowers and fruit or a box of candies, and a man his own age with a little brown mustache and a straw hat, who was struggling to reach heaven knew what destination with an ice-cream cone in either hand.

Steve did not even wonder what was happening, or how two little colored boys whom he had seen somewhere before, he did not remember where, should again have entered his world, holding hands in order not to get lost.

"It's no use my trying to question her just now, with all these visitors," said Lieutenant Murray, addressing him suddenly, as though he felt he had to account for his actions, or as though he needed his approval. "Anyway it's better to give her a little time to recover. I've asked the doctor to ask her the only question that matters at the moment."

The sister, to whom everyone was struggling to speak, no

longer concerned herself with them or with Nancy. The lieutenant held out to Steve a pack of cigarettes, then a lighted match.

"If you don't mind waiting for me here I'll drop in on my accident case. It'll save us time."

Three minutes or one hour made no difference to Steve now. Leaning against the window, he gazed in front of him with no more interest than if he had been watching fish swim in clear water, and he did not realize that the smiles of encouragement that the sister darted from time to time in his direction were intended for him.

The doctor came out of the ward, glanced up and down the corridor, looked surprised, and then went over to the sister, who spoke a few words and pointed toward the stairway down which he vanished in turn.

A young woman in hospital dress walked slowly along the corridor between the two same doorways, supported on one side by her husband, her other holding a little girl's hand, and she smiled with ecstasy, as though she were hearing celestial music. There were people everywhere, talking, going in and out, gesticulating for no apparent reason; and when at length the lieutenant appeared at the glass-paned doors at the head of the stairway, and signaled to Steve to join him, he too became a part of the general movement, relieved of having to think for himself.

"The doctor thinks, just as I do, that you'd better not see her again until this evening, maybe not till tomorrow morning. He'll let you know after his seven-o'clock visit. If you want to come with me, I have to go to my office; but I have to make a phone call first."

He went to the sister's telephone, stood by the desk, asked for his number, and Steve waited without attempting to listen to what the policeman said. He heard only words he made no sense of:

"... just as we thought, yes... Just for the record... I'm leaving right now."

Steve followed him downstairs, along the ground-floor corridor, through the entrance hall again, and out into the hospital garden, where the drives were now crowded with cars.

The sunshine, the noise, and the movement of so many people dazed him. The whole world was astir. He got mechanically into the back of the police car, while the lieutenant got in beside him and, slamming the door, said to the sergeant at the wheel:

"Headquarters."

As they drove past, Steve caught a glimpse of his own car, which no longer looked the same and seemed not to belong to him any more.

Crowds swarmed in all the streets through which they passed, mostly people in shorts, men bare to the waist, children in brightly colored swim suits; everywhere there were people eating or licking ice-cream cones, and cars sounded their horns; girls laughed, throwing back their heads or hanging on the arms of their escorts, and over it all loudspeakers spread, as it were, a coverlet of music.

"Maybe you'd like to buy one or two shirts?"

The car pulled up outside a shop with beach gear hung up in the doorway.

He was clearheaded enough to ask for two short-sleeved white shirts, tell them his size, pocket the change, and get back into the car, where the two men awaited him.

"I have a razor and everything in the office. You can clean up a little. If I don't come back with you, I'll have one of the cars take you over. The only thing is, you may have trouble finding a room."

They emerged from the town, and along the road were still other shanties selling refreshments and ice cream.

The lieutenant waited until it had become a real road, with trees on either side.

"Did you understand?" he asked when he thought the moment had come.

Steve heard the words, but it took some time before they acquired a meaning.

"Understand what?" he asked then.

"What happened to your wife."

He considered with difficulty, shook his head, and said:

"No."

He added in a lower voice:

"It's as if I scared her."

"I was the one who picked her up by the roadside last night," his companion went on, his voice more subdued. "She was lucky that some people from White Plains got car trouble not far from where she was lying. They heard her groaning. I was only a few miles away when the office notified me by radio and I got there before the ambulance."

Why did he not talk naturally? It was as though he were saying all this simply to gain time. An artificial note had crept into the conversation. Steve was not thinking of what he was saying either when he asked:

"Was she in much pain?"

"She wasn't conscious. She lost a lot of blood, which is why you found her looking so pale. She was given first-aid on the spot."

"Did they give her an injection?"

"The ambulance attendant gave her one, yes. I think so. Then we had to find a hospital with a bed available, and we tried four before——"

"I know."

"I'd have liked her to be in a private room. But it was impossible. You saw for yourself. It's annoying to interrogate her in front of the other patients."

"Yes."

Nancy's terror-stricken eyes continued to haunt him, and

still he did not ask the question. They were traveling fast; the other cars, seeing the police shield, slowed abruptly and it was like a procession. As they passed a restaurant, the lieutenant suggested:

"Would you like a cup of coffee?"

He said no. He did not have the courage to get out of the car.

"There's some in the office, anyway. You see, Hogan, the reason why your wife was frightened when she saw you is that she thinks she was responsible for what happened."

"I'm the one who took the key. She knows that."

"Just the same she went off by herself, in the dark, along the road."

Steve did not know why his companion had brought him along. He hadn't wondered about it. He was only surprised that a man like Murray should lay a hand on his knee and, without looking at him, should say in an even more expressionless voice:

"It wasn't just to steal her handbag that the man attacked her."

Steve turned toward him, his forehead wrinkled, his gaze intense, and the words seemed to come from a long way off.

"You mean that...?"

"That she was raped. That's what the doctor confirmed to us this morning at ten."

He did not move, did not see anything more, rigid, not a muscle stirring, with the pathetic picture of Nancy before his eyes. Who cared what words the lieutenant was now saying? He was right to talk. Silence must not engulf them.

"She defended herself with a lot of courage, the state of her clothing and the bruises on her body prove it. So the man hit her on the head with a heavy object, a length of lead piping, a wrench or the butt of a revolver, and she lost consciousness...."

They came onto a highway that Steve had already seen in a near or remote past, they traveled a few more miles, and then the car pulled up in front of a red-brick building of the state police.

"I thought it would be easier to talk about it on the way here. Now, let's go into my office."

Steve would not have been able to speak, he walked like a man in his sleep, he crossed a room where there were several men in uniform, and went through a doorway that was shown him.

"Excuse me a minute, will you?"

He was left alone, perhaps because the lieutenant had instructions to give or perhaps from tactfulness, but he did not weep, if that was what they had thought he would do; he did not sit down, did not walk another step; he simply opened his mouth to utter:

"Nancy!"

No sound came. Nancy had been afraid of him when he had walked over to her. It was she who was ashamed and wanted to ask forgiveness!

The door opened and the lieutenant came in with two cartons of coffee in his hands.

"It's sweet. I suppose you take sugar?"

They drank together.

"With any luck, in an hour or two we'll get him."

He went out again, this time leaving the door open, and came back almost immediately with a map of a kind Steve had never seen before, which he spread out over the table. Certain crossroads, certain strategic points in Maine and New Hampshire, not far from the Canadian border, were marked with red pencil.

"About a mile from the spot where he had to abandon your car and leave you by the side of the road, a truck driver picked him up and gave him a lift as far as Exeter. After that..."

Steve suddenly found his voice and asked harshly:

"What are you saying?"

He was almost shouting, menacingly, as though challenging the lieutenant to repeat what he had just said.

"I said that at Exeter he found——"

"Who?"

"Halligan. Right now he's somewhere in this area. . . ."

The lieutenant stretched out his arm to point to a section of the map, and Steve pulled it roughly down.

"I'm not asking where he is. I want to know if he's the one who——"

"I thought you'd understood that a long while ago."

"You're sure?"

"Yes. Since this morning, when I showed his photograph to the bartender at Armando's. He has identified him positively. Halligan left the bar around the time you were there."

His fists clenched, his jaw set, Steve continued to gaze steadily at the policeman, as though awaiting proof.

"We picked up his trail again at the log cabin where he had a drink on you and where they gave us a description of you and your car."

"Halligan!" he repeated.

"Just now at the hospital, while you were waiting in the corridor and I was down with my accident case, the doctor, at my request, showed your wife a photograph which she recognized also."

The lieutenant added after a pause:

"You understand now?"

Understand what? There were too many things to understand for one man.

"At nine o'clock this morning a garage owner called up the police from a small place in New Hampshire and gave them the number of your car's license plates, which we'd already had from the owner of the log cabin."

Had they followed his trail too, with red pencil marks on the map, as they were busy doing for Sid Halligan?

"Would you like to shave?" asked the lieutenant, opening the door of a lavatory. "There's one thing certain. Up till now all he risked for jail-breaking was an extra five or ten years. Now it's the chair!"

Steve slammed the door and, bent double, was violently sick. An acrid smell of alcohol rose up from the bowl, his throat burned, he held his stomach with both hands, eyes streaming, his whole body shaken with the spasms.

He could hear the lieutenant talking on the telephone next door, then the footsteps of two or three men, and the hum of a sort of conference taking place in the office.

It took a long time before he was able to douse his face with cold water, to smear cream over it and shave, looking as harshly at his own image as he had glared at the policeman. A terrible anger seethed in him like a tempest rumbling simultaneously at the four corners of the sky, a painful hatred only to be expressed by the word "kill," not kill with a weapon, but kill with his hands, slowly, fiercely, in full knowledge of the act, without losing a single look of terror, a twitch of agony.

The lieutenant had said:

"Now it's the chair!"

And this recalled another voice that, the night before, had also referred to that same chair, Halligan's voice saying:

"I don't want to go to the chair."

No. That wasn't quite right. The scene came back to him. Steve had asked if he had used his gun. He had asked the question in a calm voice, without indignation, with only a quiver of curiosity. And Sid had answered casually:

"If I'd fired they'd have sent me to the chair."

Wasn't it about then that Steve had thought of the two youngsters who had committed a holdup on Madison Avenue, thinking how, for ten years, they wouldn't see a single woman?

Halligan had just served four years in Sing Sing. He had not wanted to hurt the little girl he had locked in the closet with a bar of chocolate to prevent her from yelling. He had bound and gagged the mother so as to be able to search undisturbed for the household savings in the drawers. He didn't have a gun then. He also needed the husband's clothes, because he was still wearing the prison uniform. Later, he had stolen a weapon from a shopwindow. And, finally...

Stripped to the waist, his hair damp, he opened the door.

"I left the shirts in the car."

"Here they are," said the lieutenant, pointing to the package on his desk.

He was glancing quickly at Steve to judge his state of mind.

"You can put your shirt on in here. We aren't talking about anything confidential."

A sergeant was reporting on a telephone call he had just received.

"The car stolen in Exeter has been found between Woodville and Littleton, on Highway 302. The tank was empty. Either he thought he had more gas and hoped to get to the Canadian border, or else he was afraid to show himself in a garage."

The two men bent over the map.

"The New Hampshire police are keeping us informed. They've already notified the FBI. Road blocks have been set up all through the area. Because of the woods, which make it harder to track him down, they sent for bloodhounds, which they're expecting any time now."

"You hear that, Hogan?"

"Yes."

"I hope they get him before dark, and that he won't have a chance to hold up some isolated farm. After what's happened he won't hesitate to kill. He knows he's playing for keeps. O.K., that'll be all!"

The sergeant went out.

The lieutenant remained seated in front of the map. He had taken off the jacket of his uniform, and with his shirt sleeves rolled up above his elbows, he was smoking a pipe he probably never used except in the office or at home.

"Sit down. It's a bit quieter today. Most of the people have arrived wherever they were going. Tomorrow, there'll be hardly anything but local traffic, a few drownings, some dance-hall fights. It'll pick up again on Monday, when everybody starts rushing back to New York and the big towns."

Forty-five million...

He was repelled by the words, which reminded him of the motion of the car, the suction of all the wheels on the tarmac, the headlights, the miles covered in the darkness of a kind of no-man's-land, and the neon signs looming suddenly into sight.

"He threatened you with his gun?"

Steve looked straight in the eyes of the man, who, leaning back in his chair, pulled at his pipe in short little puffs.

"When I got into the car, he was sitting there and pointing his gun at me," he said, choosing his words.

Then, clipping each syllable, he added as though in defiance: "It was not necessary."

The lieutenant didn't stir, gave no sign of surprise; he asked another question:

"At the log-cabin place... By the way, it's called the Blue Moon. At the Blue Moon, as I say, did you already know who he was?"

Steve shook his head.

"I knew he was a prowler, and I guessed he was hiding. It excited me."

"Did you do all the driving?"

"We stopped somewhere at a garage to get some gas, and I bought a pint of whiskey from the attendant. I guess I drank it down in a few minutes."

He added a detail nobody was asking him for:

"Halligan had fallen asleep."

"Ah!"

"Then, we had a blowout, and he had to change the wheel

because I was no good for anything, and I just stayed slumped on the road bank. After that I don't know any more. He could have left me there or put a bullet through my head to stop me giving him away."

"Had you told him you knew who he was?"

"As we were leaving the Blue Moon."

"How do you feel now?"

"I threw up everything in my stomach. What will be done with me?"

"I'm going to have you driven back to Hayward. It's five o'clock. At seven, the doctor will examine your wife again and tell you if you can see her tonight. I suppose you plan to sleep there?"

He had not thought about it. He had not considered the question. It was the first time he had ever found himself without a bed to sleep in, with his house empty in Long Island, the children waiting for him at camp, and his wife, surrounded by five other patients, lying in a hospital bed.

"You'd be wasting your time to try the hotels and the inns. Everything is jam-packed. But there are people who, in the summer, rent out rooms by the night. You might have some luck there."

The lieutenant did not pursue the question of his relations with Halligan; he said nothing more about the matter, and that annoyed Steve. He wanted to talk about it, to confess to all the thoughts that had passed through his head during the night, sure that it would do him good, that afterward he would feel relieved. Did his companion guess what was in his mind? Did he want to avoid this confession for his own reasons? In any case he rose then and there to end the interview.

"You'd better get started right away if you don't want to sleep on the beach. Call me up when you've got an address. I'll let you know how things are going."

He called him back just as he reached the door.

"Here's your other shirt!"

Steve, who had forgotten buying two, took the package.

"I threw the dirty one in the basket," he said.

In the outer office, the same sergeant, who was listening through earphones, reported to his chief:

"The dogs have arrived and, after sniffing the seat of the abandoned car, they picked up a scent."

Steve did not want to wait, did not venture to hold out his hand.

"Thank you, Lieutenant, for the way you treated me. And for everything."

He was shown to a car with a uniformed policeman at the wheel. He got in beside him.

"Hayward. Drop him in the hospital yard, where he left his car."

The motion of the car caused him little by little to close his eyes. He fought against it for a time, then his head fell forward on his chest and he dozed off, without entirely losing the sense of where he was. Only the notion of time was obscured; events came back in a jumble to his memory, isolated images intermingled, forming and reforming new patterns.

For example, he would see Halligan, not as the nervous, thin-faced figure, but as the fair-haired man in the first bar, and he imagined Nancy with him, drinking at the counter that wasn't the one at the roadside bar but the counter at Louis's on Forty-fifth Street.

Then, he protested excitedly:

"No, that's not him! That's the wrong one!"

The real Halligan was dark-haired, sickly-looking, and his pallor was not surprising since he had spent four years in prison. He was driving the car with a mysterious smile on his lips when Steve suddenly cried:

"But it was my wife! You didn't tell me it was my wife!"

Crying the words "my wife" more and more loudly, he

grasped the man's neck in both his hands as one of the tires burst and the car came to a stop under the pine trees.

"Hey, mister..."

The policeman, smiling, was tapping him on the shoulder.

"We're here."

"I'm sorry. I guess I fell asleep. Thanks."

Most of the cars had disappeared from the hospital courtyard, and his stood alone in the middle of a great emptiness. He did not need it. Where would he go in a car? He looked up at the windows, unable to tell which was Nancy's. There was no sense in standing there staring up in the air. He must do what he had been told.

The lieutenant had advised him to look for a room first of all. There were houses quite near, most of them made of wood, painted white, with a veranda all round, and on the verandas were people, mostly old people, taking the air in their rocking chairs.

"I'm sorry to bother you, mam. You don't know where I might find a room?"

"You're the third person who's asked me that in the last half hour. Try the house at the corner. They haven't anything left, but they might know of something."

He saw the sea, quite close, at the end of a street. The sun had not yet disappeared in the opposite direction, behind the houses and trees, but the surface of the water was already a chilly green.

"Excuse me, mam, do you——"

"You're looking for a room?"

"My wife's in the hospital, and..."

He was sent elsewhere, and again elsewhere, into streets farther and farther away from the center of town, where the people sat on their doorsteps.

"Just for yourself?"

"Yes. My wife's in the hospital..."

"You had an accident?"

They found it strange that he had no car.

"I left my car over there. I'll go and get it as soon as I find a place to stay."

"All we can offer you is a camp bed on the back porch. It's a screened porch, but I warn you it won't be warm. I'll give you two blankets."

"That'll do fine."

"I have to charge you four dollars."

He paid in advance. Almost directly after letting him have that money the garage proprietor had thought it his duty to notify the police. Steve had not suspected, as he drove toward Hayward, that they knew exactly where he was.

Instead of disturbing him, the thought rather reassured him. It was comforting to find that the world was well organized, society well knit.

The police couldn't prevent everything. Nancy hadn't been able either to stop him drinking last night. She had tried all she could, and it was she in the end who had paid.

"What time do you expect to be back?"

"I don't know. I must go to the hospital and see my wife. I won't be late."

"At ten, I go to bed and lock the door. I'm warning you. Fill in your form."

Writing his name made him think of the news item in the paper. There would be more about the attack in the evening papers, inevitably. The radio must have already announced that the victim had been identified. He had often read news of that sort without attaching any importance to the words, *"the victim was raped."*

Everyone would know. He thought of Mr. Schwartz, of the switchboard girl who took a secret pleasure in telling him that his wife was in conference, of Louis and his five-o'clock customers. And then to his distress, so apparent that his landlady eyed him with some misgiving, was added pity of a special kind. It was not only as her husband that he pictured Nancy. He thought about her as about a woman walking in the street, in daily life, a woman after whom people gazed, murmuring sadly:

"Is she the one who was raped?"

This gave rise to new problems. Perhaps Nancy, lying alone in her bed, had already faced them? In knowing her as he did, it seemed to him that she would never agree to meet the people they knew or return to her former life.

"If you're going to the hospital and want a short cut, take your first right and keep walking till you come to a restaurant with its front painted blue. You can see the hospital from there."

What would be wonderful would be for them to live quite alone, just the two of them and the children, without seeing a soul, not even Dick and his wife, who always wore a jaundiced smile and was jealous of Nancy anyway. Nancy would stay at home. He would go to work as usual, because he had to earn his living, but he'd come straight back without dropping in at Louis's and without ever wanting a martini. No one would ask them any questions, or make any remarks.

The noise and the blare of music from the center of town came to him, muffled by distance; radios were going in a good many of the houses, and in others one could make out motionless figures in a half-light, in front of the lunar pallor of the television screen.

He reached the restaurant with a blue-painted front and went in, not for a drink, but to get something to eat, because he had cramp in his stomach. In any case, there was no bar. They did not serve alcoholic drinks. He would not have been tempted anyway. If they let him talk to Nancy that evening, and if she were not too exhausted, he intended to swear to her, then and there, that he would never again touch a drop of alcohol; and he was firmly resolved to keep the promise, not only for her sake, but for his own.

A girl smelling of perspiration wiped the table in front of him with a dirty cloth, and, thrusting a menu into his hand, stood awaiting his order with her pencil poised.

"Just bring me anything—a sandwich."

"Why not lobster salad? That's today's special."

"Will it be quicker?"

"It's all ready. Coffee?"

"Please."

An afternoon paper was lying on a nearby table, but he preferred not to look at it. The clock on the wall pointed to ten-past six. At that hour yesterday his wife and he had still been in their home. So as not to waste time they had not sat down to eat their sandwiches, and he could hear again the hum of the refrigerator as his wife had opened it to take out a Coca-Cola.

"Do you want one?"

He could not tell her that he had just had a rye. That was where it had all started. She was wearing the green summer suit she had bought on Fifth Avenue, never dreaming that the Boston papers would be talking about it next morning.

"Ketchup?"

He was impatient to get back to the hospital. Even if they didn't let him go up right away, he would feel nearer to her. Besides at the hospital he was not tempted to think. He did not want to think any more today. His weariness had reached the point where it set up an ache throughout his body, as though inside the bones. It had happened to him often enough to be up all night, even to be up drinking all night, and to feel sick in the morning, but he had nearly always pulled himself together with the help of alcohol. It would probably have worked this evening, too. That morning, the scotch had enabled him to bear up and drive here, and had even steadied his nerves enough to enable him to telephone all over and find Nancy.

He was sorry the waitress in the cafeteria was not here to give him support. Everyone in this place was in a hurry, there was a constant clatter of dishes, the girls bustled about without being able to satisfy the customers, and there was always some noise lover to put five cents in the juke-box.

"Dessert? There's apple pie and lemon-meringue pie."

He preferred to pay and go. All the windows in the hospital were lit up, and if Nancy had not been on the side of the door he might have been able to see her bed. Not all the curtains were drawn. One caught a glimpse here and there of a nurse's white cap, or the outline of a patient bent over a magazine.

As he passed his car he looked away uneasily because of all it brought to mind, and he resolved to trade it for another, even an older one, if he got the chance.

He had forgotten to call the lieutenant, who had asked him to do so. He remembered seeing a phone booth in the hospital entrance hall. As soon as he had any news, he would have to telephone the Keanes as well. He must not forget the children. But first he needed to have a clearer idea of what they were going to do.

"You don't know if I may see my wife?"

The girl recognized him and put a plug in the switchboard.

"It's the husband of the patient in Twenty-two. You know who I mean? Yes. What? The doctor's not due before seven? I'll tell him."

She repeated:

"Not before seven."

"May I use the phone?"

"The one in the booth is public."

He rang police headquarters.

"This is Steve Hogan. I'd like to speak to Lieutenant Murray?"

"This is the trooper who was with him at the hospital, Mr. Hogan. I know all about it. The lieutenant's out to dinner."

"He asked me to call up and give him my address here."

"You found a room?"

He read out the address his landlady had written on a scrap of paper.

"Is there any news?"

"We've had some in the past half hour."

The voice was happy.

"It's all over. At first, the dogs went off on a wrong scent, and that wasted an hour. So they were brought back to the car, and that time they got it right."

"Did he put up a fight?"

"When he saw he was cornered he threw his gun away and put his hands up. He was scared green and kept on begging them not to hurt him. The FBI took charge of him. They'll come here tomorrow when they bring him back to Sing Sing."

"Thank you."

"Good night. You can tell your wife the news. She'll be pleased too."

He left the booth and went and sat down in a chair in the hall, where he was alone. Through the glass pane he could see the upper half of the receptionist's face as she sat typing and occasionally glancing curiously in his direction.

He did not at first recognize the doctor, who came from outside and whom he had not yet seen in ordinary clothes, but the doctor knew him, nearly passed him by, then turned back to him, worried.

Steve rose.

"Don't get up."

The doctor sat down beside him, resting his elbows on his knees as though for a quiet man-to-man talk.

"The lieutenant told you?"

Steve nodded.

"I suppose you realize that she's the one for whom it's the most tragic. I haven't seen her yet this evening. The head wound isn't nice, but that heals rapidly. By the way, you'd better know, so that you don't hurt her by looking shocked, that we had to cut off her hair and shave her head."

"I understand, Doctor."

"We can't keep her here long, turning away urgent cases as we've done all day. Do you have a good doctor? Where do you live?"

"On Long Island."

"Is there a hospital nearby?"

"About three miles away."

"I'll see just how she is and if she'll soon be able to make the trip without risk. The most important thing, in her case, is her state of mind, and that's up to you. Wait a minute! I'm sure you're ready to give her all the care in the world. Unfortunately this isn't the first such case that I've had to attend. The reaction is always violent. It will be a long time before your wife considers herself a normal person again, or reacts like a normal person, particularly after all the publicity that there'll be about her, which no one can prevent. If they catch her attacker there'll be a trial."

"He's been arrested."

"You'll have to be patient, resourceful, and if her progress is slow you may have to call in a specialist."

He got to his feet.

"You may come up with me and wait in the corridor. Provided there's nothing new, I'll only be a minute or two. I think she told me you have children?"

"Two. We were on our way to Maine, where they're waiting for us to take them home from camp."

"I'll talk to you about them later."

They went up. The sister at the desk wasn't the one Steve knew, and the doctor exchanged a few words with her.

"Just take a seat . . ."

"Thanks."

He preferred to remain standing. The corridors were empty, bathed in a soft yellow light. The doctor had gone into Nancy's ward.

"Did she sleep?"

"I don't know. I came on duty at six."

She glanced at a record sheet. "I can tell you that she took some bouillon, some meat and vegetables."

The words had a reassuring sound.

"Have you seen her?"

"Last night, when they brought her in."

He didn't press the matter, preferring not to know the details. From the nearest doorway came the monotonous murmur of a conversation between two women.

The doctor appeared and called:

"Nurse, will you come here a minute?"

He said a few words and she went into the ward as the doctor came toward Steve.

"You'll see her. The nurse will let you know when she's ready. Unless there are complications, which I don't expect, there's no reason why she shouldn't leave on Tuesday. The weekend will be over and the roads won't be so congested."

"Will she need an ambulance?"

"If you have a good car and drive without shaking her too much it won't be necessary. I'll see her before she goes. I'm telling you now so that you can make arrangements. As for the children, if you have someone to look after them at home..."

"We have a part-time baby-sitter and I can ask her to stay longer."

"It will help your wife's recovery if life around her can be as normal as possible right from the start. Don't stay with her now more than twenty or thirty minutes, and don't let her tire herself talking."

"I promise, Doctor."

The sister reappeared, but still not for him. She had come to get something he couldn't quite see out of her handbag, which was in a cupboard, and then she went back into the ward.

A good ten minutes dragged by and at last she beckoned to him from the doorway.

"She's waiting for you," she said, standing aside for him to pass.

A screen had been put around the bed to separate it from the rest of the room, and there was a chair beside it. Nancy kept her eyes closed, but she was not asleep, and he could see quivers passing over her face. He noticed that her lips were redder, spied traces of powder near the bandage that circled her head, about level with her ears.

Without a word he sat down, and his hand reached for the hand lying on the sheet.

8

WITHOUT opening her eyes, she whispered: "Don't say anything. . . ."

Then she herself was silent, motionless, except for her hand, which moved in Steve's hand the better to nestle in it. They were both in an oasis of peace and silence where no sound reached them save the hissing breath of the woman with fever.

Steve avoided even the least movement, and it was Nancy who presently said in a voice that was still very low:

"First, I want you to know that I didn't ask for the powder and lipstick. The nurse did it. She insisted for fear I'd scare you."

He opened his mouth but did not speak, and finally closed his eyes too, because they were even closer together that way, not seeing one another, with only the touch of their intertwined fingers.

"You aren't too tired?"

"No . . . You see, Nancy——"

"Ssh! Don't move. I can feel your pulse beating."

This time she remained silent so long that he thought she had fallen asleep. But at last she said:

"I'm very old now. I was already two years older than you. Since last night, I'm an old woman. Don't say anything. Let me talk. I've done a lot of thinking this afternoon. They gave me another injection but I managed to stay awake and I was able to think."

He had never felt so close to her. It was as though a circle of light and warmth surrounded them, giving them shelter from the rest of the world, and in their joined hands their pulses were beating with the same rhythm.

"In a few hours I've aged at least ten years. Don't be impatient. You must let me finish."

It was at once good and heart-rending to hear her, talking always in a whisper, so that it might be more secret, more intimately theirs; her voice had no expression, and she made long pauses between the sentences.

"You've got to understand, Steve, if you haven't thought it out for yourself yet, that our whole life will be changed, that from now on nothing will ever be the same again. I will never be a woman like other women, I will never be your wife again."

And as she sensed he was going to protest, she hurried on to stop him.

"Ssh!... I want you to listen and to understand. There are things that can't exist any more, because, each time, the thought of what happened..."

"Don't!..."

He had opened his eyes, and he saw her with her eyelids still closed, with her lower lip trembling in a slight pout as it did when she was going to cry.

"No, Steve! You couldn't either. I know what I'm saying. You know it too, but you're trying to deceive yourself. For me, it's finished. There's a kind of life I shall never know again."

Her throat tight, she swallowed, and he thought he caught, for an instant, the gleam of her eyes beneath the fluttering lids.

"I won't ask you to stay with me. You'll go on living a normal life. We'll do the best we can to make it easy."

"Nancy!"

"Sssh!... Let me finish, Steve. Sooner or later, you'd find out for yourself the things I'm saying this evening, and then it would be much harder for both of us. That's why I wanted you to know right away. I was waiting for you."

He didn't know he was crushing her hand, and she moaned:

"You're hurting me."

"I'm sorry."

"It's silly, isn't it? A person doesn't realize until it's too late. When people are happy, they think nothing of it, do foolish things, even rebel at times. We've been happy, the four of us."

And then, suddenly, he forgot the doctor's warning, forgot to think, forgot the wound on Nancy's head, the hospital ward where they were. A tide of warmth had welled up in his breast and words came crowding into his mind that he had to speak to her, words he had never spoken to her and perhaps never even thought.

"It's not true!" he protested at once, as she had just spoken of their past happiness.

"Steve!"

"I believe I've done some thinking too, without knowing it. And what you just said is a lie. It's not as though we were happy yesterday."

"Don't! . . ."

His voice was as thick as his wife's and yet he managed to give it a restrained vehemence that was the more eloquent.

This was not how he had imagined their talk together and he had never thought that he would one day tell her the things he was about to say. He felt himself to be in a state of utter sincerity, and it was as though he were naked, as sensitive as if the skin had been stripped off him.

"Don't look at me! Keep your eyes shut. Just listen to me. The proof that we weren't happy is that, the minute we strayed from our everyday routine, from our ordinary habits, I felt so lost that I had a violent need to drink. And you, you needed, each day, to go to an office on Madison Avenue to convince yourself that you had an interesting life. How many times have we stayed alone together, at home, without feeling the need, after a few minutes, to pick up a magazine or listen to the radio?"

Nancy's eyelids were damp at the lashes, her lips pouted more and more; he had nearly let go her hand, and she clung to his nervously.

"Do you know just when it was, yesterday, that I started to betray you? You were still in the house. We hadn't yet started. I told you I was going to fill up the gas tank."

She murmured:

"You had first talked about getting cigarettes."

Her face had already lightened.

"It was to have a rye. I stayed on rye all night. I wanted to feel strong and uninhibited."

"You hated me."

"You too!"

Didn't the trace of a smile appear on her lips as she whispered:

"Yes."

"So I continued to rebel all by myself until I woke up this morning at the edge of a road where I didn't remember stopping."

"You had an accident?"

He had the feeling that, for the first time since they had known one another, there was no deception between them any longer, nothing more, nothing as thick even as a veil, to prevent them being themselves face-to-face.

"Not an accident. It's my turn to say that you've got to know, and right now. I met a man in whom, for hours, I tried to see another me, another me that wasn't a coward, a man I wished I could be like; and I spilled out everything that was on my mind, all the rottenness fermenting inside me. I told him about you, perhaps about the children as well, and I may even have said I didn't love them. Yet I knew who that man was and where he came from!"

He had shut his eyes again.

"I had a drunkard's determination to soil everything, and the man I confided in like that was..."

He scarcely heard that she repeated:

"Don't..."

He had finished. He wept in silence, and the tears running down from beneath his closed lids were not bitter. Nancy's hand lay inert in his.

"Do you understand, now...?"

He had to wait for the tightness in his throat to pass.

"Do you understand that it's only today we will begin to live?"

Opening his eyes, he was surprised to find that she was looking at him.

Had she been watching him all the time he was talking?

"That's all. You see, you were right to say that, since yesterday, we've come a long way."

He thought he caught a last hint of incredulity in her eyes.

"It'll be a different life. I don't know what it will be like, but I'm sure we'll be living it together."

She still tried not to give in.

"Is it true?" she asked with a candor that he did not recognize in her.

The sister passed behind him to attend to the fever patient, who must have rung for her. All the time she stayed in the room, they avoided talking.

It did not matter now. Perhaps when he got back into everyday life Steve would feel slightly embarrassed at the recollection of this outburst. But wasn't he still more ashamed when he woke up the morning after holding forth as a drunkard?

They gazed at one another unself-consciously, each feeling that this moment would probably never come again. Each strained toward the other, but this was apparent only in their eyes, locked in a gaze in which grew a look of grave enchantment.

"O.K., folks?" called the sister as she was leaving.

The vulgarity of the words did not disturb them.

"Five minutes more and that's all!" she announced, going out of the door with a bedpan covered with a cloth in her hand.

Three of the five minutes had elapsed when Nancy spoke, her voice firmer than before:

"You're sure, Steve?"

"And you?" he answered with a smile.

"Maybe we can try."

The thing that mattered was not what was going to happen but that this minute should have existed, and already he was trying not to lose its warmth; he wanted to leave quickly, because anything they might say could only weaken their emotion.

"May I kiss you?"

She nodded and he stood up, bent over her, put his lips cautiously to hers, and pressed them. The two remained thus for several seconds, and when he stood upright Nancy's hand still clung to his own; he had to loosen her fingers one by one before hurrying to the door without looking back.

He almost failed to hear when the sister called to him. He had not seen her as he passed close by.

"Mr. Hogan!"

He stopped, saw her smiling at him.

"I'm sorry to break in on you like that. I just wanted to tell you that from now on you must only come during visiting hours, which are posted downstairs. We made an exception this time because it was the first day."

Seeing him glance toward Nancy's ward, she added:

"Don't worry. I'll see that she sleeps all right. By the way, the doctor gave me these for you. Take both of them when you go to bed and you'll have a good night."

There were two tablets in a small white envelope, which he slipped into his pocket.

"Thanks."

The night was clear and the stones of the courtyard shone beneath the moon. He got mechanically into his car and drove, not toward his lodgings, but toward the sea. He still needed to live a little while with the things he felt inside him, upon which the lights of the town, the music, the shooting galleries, the swings had no hold. All that surrounded him had no substance, no reality. He drove along a street that grew darker as he went and at the end of it he found a rock with the sea lapping almost soundlessly against it.

A cooler air came from the open sea, a rich scent with which he filled his lungs. Without shutting the door of the car behind him he walked to the extreme edge of the rock, stopping only when the water touched the tips of his shoes, and furtively, as though he were ashamed, he repeated the gesture he had made as a child when for the first time he had been taken to see the ocean, bending down and dabbling his hand in the water, keeping it there for a long time to enjoy its living freshness.

Then he waited no longer, looked for the blue-fronted restaurant that served him as a landmark, and found the road along which he had walked, and the house where he was to sleep.

The landlady and her husband were sitting together in the darkness of the veranda, and he did not see them until he had started up the steps.

"You're early, Mr. Hogan. To be sure, you wouldn't have the heart to be enjoying yourself. You have no suitcase? Wait, I'll switch on a light in the house."

A very white bulb suddenly lit up the flowered wallpaper in the hall.

"I won't let you sleep in your clothes after what you've been through."

She knew, now, and she spoke to him as one does to someone bereft.

"How's your poor wife?"

"Better."

"What a shock it must have been for her! Men like that ought to be shot down without taking the trouble to try them. If anything like that happened to my daughter I think I'd be capable..."

He would have to get used to it. Nancy too. It would be a part of their new life, at least for a time. He waited patiently for the woman to finish and then she went into her bedroom for a pair of her husband's pajamas.

"They may be a bit short, but it's better than nothing. If you'll come with me I'll show you the bathroom."

She was switching on lights, bringing one room after another out of darkness.

"I found you a third blanket. It's a cotton one, but it'll be some help. You'll appreciate it toward morning, when the dampness comes in with the mist from the sea."

He was in a hurry to get to bed, to withdraw into himself. But he got out again when he remembered the doctor's tablets, and went to get a glass of water to take them with. The low, muffled voices of the couple came to him from the front of the house, but he paid no attention.

"Good night, Nancy," he said in a whisper recalling the hospital ward.

There were crickets in the garden. Later, there was an opening and shutting of doors, heavy footsteps went up the stairs to the first floor, someone struggled violently to open or close a window that seemed to be jammed—and all he remembered of the night was a sensation of cold creeping into him, against which the blankets were useless.

He had no dreams, nor did he awake until the sun was shining directly on him and he felt his face almost scorched. The town was already full of movement and voices, cars were passing along the street, cocks were crowing somewhere, and a clatter of crockery came from within the house.

He had left his clothes hanging on the bathroom door, with his watch in them. When he went into the hall, his landlady called from the kitchen:

"Well, you certainly slept well! You can't say fresh air doesn't agree with you!"

"What time is it?"

"Half-past nine. I expect you'd like some coffee? I've just made some. By the way, the police lieutenant called in to see you."

"What time was it?"

"About eight. He was in a hurry because he was going to the hospital with someone. I told him you were asleep, and he wouldn't let me wake you. He said he'll be in his office all morning and you can go there any time you like."

"Did you see who was with him?"

"I didn't dare have a look. There were three men in the back of the car, all in plain clothes, and I could swear the one in the middle was handcuffed. I shouldn't be surprised if it was the man they caught in New Hampshire who's in the paper this morning, the one that escaped from prison two days ago and managed to do so much harm in such a short time. You know about it. Do you want the paper?"

It must have surprised her that he should say no. She must have thought him cold, but his calm was not coldness. He went into the kitchen to drink the cup of coffee she poured for him, then had a shower and shaved; and when he came out on to the veranda some women neighbors were at their windows or on their doorsteps to look at him.

"May I spend tonight here again?"

"As many nights as you like. I'm only sorry it's not more comfortable."

He drove into the town and stopped to have breakfast at the restaurant where he had dined the night before. When he had finished eating and had drunk two more cups of coffee he went into the phone booth, asked for the number of Walla Walla Camp, and waited nearly five minutes, staring through the glass pane at the counter, behind which eggs were being fried by the dozen.

"Mrs. Keane? This is Steve Hogan."

"It's you, poor Mr. Hogan? We worried a lot all day yesterday in spite of your phone call. We were wondering what had happened to you. It was only in the evening that we learned about your wife's misfortune. How is she, poor dear? Are you near her? Have you seen her?"

"She's getting on all right, thank you, Mrs. Keane. I'm in Hayward. I'm planning to come up and get the children tomorrow. You haven't told them anything?"

"Only that their mummy and daddy were held up. Imagine, Bonnie said you must be having a very good time on the trip! Do you want to speak to them?"

"No. I'd rather not say anything over the phone. Just tell them I'll be there tomorrow."

"What are you going to do?"

And still he did not grow impatient.

"We'll go back home Tuesday, when the roads are clearer."

"Will your wife be fit to stand the trip?"

"The doctor's sure of it."

"To think that a thing like that should have happened to her! All the parents who come tell us about it, and if you only knew how sorry they are for you both. Well, it could have been even worse..."

He surprised himself by replying indifferently:

"Yes."

He could not go to Maine, come back, then pick up Nancy and return to Long Island in a single day, except by driving like mad. The children would have to spend a night in Hayward. Luckily on Monday night everyone would be gone, and he would easily find hotel accommodation.

He thought of everything, for example, that he would not need to tell Mr. Schwartz that Nancy would not be at the office on Tuesday morning, because by now he would know the news from the papers. The same applied to his own boss. He could simply send a wire the next day, which would reach Madison Avenue first thing on Tuesday, saying, "Returning office Thursday."

He was allowing himself Wednesday in which to organize the household. He could not make arrangements any earlier with Ida, their colored girl, because she had told them that she was going to spend the weekend with relations in Baltimore.

He was clearing things up, little by little, trying to think of everything, including the story he would tell the two children, which must not depart from the truth more than was absolutely necessary because they would hear their school friends talk.

He looked forward to seeing them again. But not in the same way as he had at other times. There was a new sort of closeness between them and him now; Bonnie and Dan, too, would be part of their new life.

After his two-o'clock visit to the hospital he would see about trading the car. There was certainly a used-car dealer's somewhere, and those places do more trade over the weekends than on any other days. And he must not forget to ask the lieutenant to draw up a temporary paper, some kind of certificate to replace his driver's license, unless, perhaps, his wallet had been recovered.

There was yet another thing to do, much more important, which he could not postpone. He was calm. It was essential that he should retain all his self-control. He drove right on to the highway without having the curiosity to switch on the radio, and it was half-past ten when he pulled up outside the police building. One of the cars by the entrance, which bore New Hampshire license plates but no other distinctive sign, must be the one in which the FBI detectives had brought Sid Halligan.

It was also necessary that he should grow accustomed to hearing this name, to speaking it in his own mind. The weather was as fine as the previous day, but a little more oppressive, with a slight haze in the air that could lead to a thunderstorm toward the end of the day.

He crushed his cigarette under the sole of his shoe before going up the flight of stone steps and into the outer office, where one of the policemen was busy questioning a couple. The woman, her make-up smudged, had the voice and manner of a cabaret singer.

"Is the lieutenant in his office?"

"Step right in, Mr. Hogan. I'll tell him you're here."

In the time it took him to reach the door, which he knew from before, he had been announced over the intercom system, so a hand pulled at the door at the very moment he pushed it. Lieutenant Murray greeted him, seemed a little surprised by his attitude.

"Come in, Hogan. I thought you'd come. I needn't ask if you slept well. Take a seat."

Steve shook his head as he looked about him. He said in a quieter voice than usual:

"He's here?"

The policeman nodded, still surprised, perhaps at finding him so composed.

"Can I see him?"

The lieutenant in his turn became more grave.

"You'll see him in a moment, Hogan. But first I insist that you sit down for a few minutes."

He did so, obediently, and listened in the same way as he had listened to the landlady and to the condolences of Mrs.

Keane. The other man felt it so keenly that he spoke without conviction, filling his pipe with short taps of his index finger.

"He was brought here last night, and right away this morning we took him to Hayward. I didn't want to speak to you about it yesterday, and I hope you aren't angry at me. It was better to get a formal identification right now. In an hour, the FBI men will start off with him for Sing Sing. If it hadn't taken place this morning, your wife would have had to later on, and——"

"How was my wife?"

"We found her remarkably self-possessed."

Steve could not quite repress the smile that rose to his lips unbidden, and seemed to take the lieutenant aback.

"At six o'clock this morning, a private room in the hospital became free, and I arranged for her to be transferred."

"Someone died during the night?"

The change in him must indeed be considerable, because he had hardly to open his mouth, and the lieutenant would practically lose his poise.

Without answering the question he asked in his turn:

"You had a talk with your wife yesterday evening?"

"We straightened things out," Steve said simply.

"I guessed as much this morning. She seemed at peace. First, I went alone into the room to ask her if she felt strong enough to stand the identification. As a precaution, the doctor waited all the time in the corridor, just in case. Contrary to what I'd expected, she was neither nervous nor afraid. She said as naturally as you're talking to me this morning:

"'I suppose it's got to be done, Lieutenant?'

"I said yes. Then she asked where you were, and I said you were still asleep, and she seemed pleased. She said:

"'Do be quick.'

"I motioned to the detectives to bring in the prisoner. Ever since his arrest he's denied the assault and claimed mistaken identity. He admits everything else, which is less serious. I expected that. When he came into the room, he held his head high, and he started to grin insolently. Standing in the middle of the room, he stared at your wife, taunting her.

"She didn't move. Her expression didn't change. After a moment she frowned, as though to see him better.

"'Do you recognize him?' one of the detectives asked, while the other took down shorthand notes.

"She merely said:

"'It's him.'

"He still stared at her with the same look of defiance while the FBI man went down the list of questions which each time your wife answered with a distinct:

"'Yes.'

"That's all, Hogan. All told, it took less than ten minutes. Reporters and photographers were waiting in the corridor. When Halligan had left the room and only then, I asked your wife if I could let them in, warned her that it's never a good idea to get on the wrong side of the Press. She answered:

"'If the doctor doesn't mind, let them in.'

"The doctor allowed only the photographers in, just for a few minutes, forbidding the reporters to go and question her.

"She was brave, I can tell you. I don't mind admitting that before I left I couldn't help shaking her hand."

Steve looked straight in front of him, saying nothing.

"I don't know whether she'll have to appear in person when the case goes before the jury. Anyway, there are enough charges, and they're so complicated, that it'll take some weeks; and by then your wife will have recovered. Maybe the court will even be satisfied with an affidavit."

The lieutenant looked more and more embarrassed. Watch Steve as he might, he didn't understand. It seemed to be beyond him.

"Do you still want to see him?"

"Yes."

"Now?"

"As soon as possible."

Murray left him alone. Steve got to his feet and stood facing the window, as though collecting himself.

He heard the sound of coming and going in the corridors, the opening of doors, the footsteps of several people. After a rather long time the lieutenant came in first, leaving the door open, and went over to sit at his desk.

The first to enter the room then was Sid Halligan, his wrists linked by the handcuffs, and behind him came the two FBI men.

Everyone except the lieutenant remained standing. Someone had shut the door.

Steve still faced the window, his head low, his fists clenched at the end of his hanging arms. The blood had left his face. There were beads of sweat on his forehead and his upper lip.

They saw him close his eyes, steel himself as though he needed all his strength, and then, slowly, he turned partly around and faced Halligan.

The lieutenant, who was watching them both, saw the gradual disintegration of the smile on the prisoner's face.

For a moment he feared he would have to intervene; he even moved ever so slightly in his chair, because Steve, whose eyes seemed unable to detach themselves from those of his wife's aggressor, had begun to stiffen, his body had grown hard, his jaw had started to jut.

The right fist moved an inch or two and Halligan, who was aware of it, quickly raised his arms fettered in the handcuffs, and threw a frightened look at his guards, as though calling them to his rescue.

They had not spoken a word. Not a sound had been heard. Once again, Steve relaxed, the lines of his body became rounder, his shoulders sagged slowly, his face blurred.

"I'm sorry..." he stammered.

And the others did not know whether it was for the gesture he had barely avoided.

He could look Halligan in the face, now, with the expression he had a moment before when the lieutenant was talking to him, the expression that was his since the previous evening.

He gazed at him for a long time, as he had decided to force himself to, because it had seemed to him compulsory before trying out their new life.

No one suspected that it was some part of himself that he had nearly struck when he had raised his fist, or that it was something of his own past that he outfaced in the prisoner's eyes.

Now, he had seen the end of the road. He could look elsewhere, return to everyday life; he looked about him, surprised to find them all so tense, and said in his normal voice:

"That's all."

He added:

"Thank you, Lieutenant."

If they had questions to ask him, he was ready. It did not matter any more.

Nancy, too, had been brave.

Shadow Rock Farm
Lakeville, Connecticut
14 July, 1953

OTHER NEW YORK REVIEW CLASSICS*

J.R. ACKERLEY Hindoo Holiday
J.R. ACKERLEY My Dog Tulip
J.R. ACKERLEY My Father and Myself
CÉLESTE ALBARET Monsieur Proust
DANTE ALIGHIERI The Inferno
DANTE ALIGHIERI The New Life
WILLIAM ATTAWAY Blood on the Forge
W.H. AUDEN (EDITOR) The Living Thoughts of Kierkegaard
W.H. AUDEN W.H. Auden's Book of Light Verse
ERICH AUERBACH Dante: Poet of the Secular World
DOROTHY BAKER Cassandra at the Wedding
J.A. BAKER The Peregrine
HONORÉ DE BALZAC The Unknown Masterpiece *and* Gambara
MAX BEERBOHM Seven Men
STEPHEN BENATAR Wish Her Safe at Home
FRANS G. BENGTSSON The Long Ships
ALEXANDER BERKMAN Prison Memoirs of an Anarchist
GEORGES BERNANOS Mouchette
ADOLFO BIOY CASARES Asleep in the Sun
ADOLFO BIOY CASARES The Invention of Morel
CAROLINE BLACKWOOD Corrigan
CAROLINE BLACKWOOD Great Granny Webster
NICOLAS BOUVIER The Way of the World
MALCOLM BRALY On the Yard
MILLEN BRAND The Outward Room
JOHN HORNE BURNS The Gallery
ROBERT BURTON The Anatomy of Melancholy
CAMARA LAYE The Radiance of the King
GIROLAMO CARDANO The Book of My Life
DON CARPENTER Hard Rain Falling
J.L. CARR A Month in the Country
BLAISE CENDRARS Moravagine
EILEEN CHANG Love in a Fallen City
UPAMANYU CHATTERJEE English, August: An Indian Story
ANTON CHEKHOV Peasants and Other Stories
RICHARD COBB Paris and Elsewhere
COLETTE The Pure and the Impure
JOHN COLLIER Fancies and Goodnights
CARLO COLLODI The Adventures of Pinocchio
IVY COMPTON-BURNETT A House and Its Head
IVY COMPTON-BURNETT Manservant and Maidservant
BARBARA COMYNS The Vet's Daughter
EVAN S. CONNELL The Diary of a Rapist
ALBERT COSSERY The Jokers
ASTOLPHE DE CUSTINE Letters from Russia
LORENZO DA PONTE Memoirs
ELIZABETH DAVID A Book of Mediterranean Food
ELIZABETH DAVID Summer Cooking
L.J. DAVIS A Meaningful Life

* *For a complete list of titles, visit www.nyrb.com or write to:*
Catalog Requests, NYRB, 435 Hudson Street, New York, NY 10014

VIVANT DENON No Tomorrow/Point de lendemain
MARIA DERMOÛT The Ten Thousand Things
DER NISTER The Family Mashber
TIBOR DÉRY Niki: The Story of a Dog
ARTHUR CONAN DOYLE The Exploits and Adventures of Brigadier Gerard
CHARLES DUFF A Handbook on Hanging
BRUCE DUFFY The World As I Found It
DAPHNE DU MAURIER Don't Look Now: Stories
ELAINE DUNDY The Dud Avocado
ELAINE DUNDY The Old Man and Me
G.B. EDWARDS The Book of Ebenezer Le Page
MARCELLUS EMANTS A Posthumous Confession
EURIPIDES Grief Lessons: Four Plays; translated by Anne Carson
J.G. FARRELL Troubles
J.G. FARRELL The Siege of Krishnapur
J.G. FARRELL The Singapore Grip
ELIZA FAY Original Letters from India
KENNETH FEARING The Big Clock
FÉLIX FÉNÉON Novels in Three Lines
M.I. FINLEY The World of Odysseus
MASANOBU FUKUOKA The One-Straw Revolution
CARLO EMILIO GADDA That Awful Mess on the Via Merulana
MAVIS GALLANT The Cost of Living: Early and Uncollected Stories
MAVIS GALLANT Paris Stories
MAVIS GALLANT Varieties of Exile
GABRIEL GARCÍA MÁRQUEZ Clandestine in Chile: The Adventures of Miguel Littín
THÉOPHILE GAUTIER My Fantoms
JEAN GENET Prisoner of Love
JOHN GLASSCO Memoirs of Montparnasse
P.V. GLOB The Bog People: Iron-Age Man Preserved
EDMOND AND JULES DE GONCOURT Pages from the Goncourt Journals
EDWARD GOREY (EDITOR) The Haunted Looking Glass
A.C. GRAHAM Poems of the Late T'ang
WILLIAM LINDSAY GRESHAM Nightmare Alley
EMMETT GROGAN Ringolevio: A Life Played for Keeps
VASILY GROSSMAN Everything Flows
VASILY GROSSMAN Life and Fate
VASILY GROSSMAN The Road
OAKLEY HALL Warlock
PATRICK HAMILTON The Slaves of Solitude
PATRICK HAMILTON Twenty Thousand Streets Under the Sky
PETER HANDKE Short Letter, Long Farewell
PETER HANDKE Slow Homecoming
PETER HANDKE A Sorrow Beyond Dreams
ELIZABETH HARDWICK The New York Stories of Elizabeth Hardwick
ELIZABETH HARDWICK Seduction and Betrayal
ELIZABETH HARDWICK Sleepless Nights
L.P. HARTLEY The Go-Between
GILBERT HIGHET Poets in a Landscape
JANET HOBHOUSE The Furies
HUGO VON HOFMANNSTHAL The Lord Chandos Letter
JAMES HOGG The Private Memoirs and Confessions of a Justified Sinner

RICHARD HOLMES Shelley: The Pursuit
ALISTAIR HORNE A Savage War of Peace: Algeria 1954–1962
RICHARD HUGHES A High Wind in Jamaica
RICHARD HUGHES In Hazard
RICHARD HUGHES The Fox in the Attic (The Human Predicament, Vol. 1)
RICHARD HUGHES The Wooden Shepherdess (The Human Predicament, Vol. 2)
MAUDE HUTCHINS Victorine
YASUSHI INOUE Tun-huang
HENRY JAMES The Ivory Tower
HENRY JAMES The New York Stories of Henry James
HENRY JAMES The Other House
HENRY JAMES The Outcry
TOVE JANSSON The Summer Book
TOVE JANSSON The True Deceiver
RANDALL JARRELL (EDITOR) Randall Jarrell's Book of Stories
DAVID JONES In Parenthesis
ERNST JÜNGER The Glass Bees
FRIGYES KARINTHY A Journey Round My Skull
YASHAR KEMAL Memed, My Hawk
MURRAY KEMPTON Part of Our Time: Some Ruins and Monuments of the Thirties
DAVID KIDD Peking Story
DEZSŐ KOSZTOLÁNYI Skylark
TÉTÉ-MICHEL KPOMASSIE An African in Greenland
GYULA KRÚDY Sunflower
SIGIZMUND KRZHIZHANOVSKY Memories of the Future
PATRICK LEIGH FERMOR Between the Woods and the Water
PATRICK LEIGH FERMOR Mani: Travels in the Southern Peloponnese
PATRICK LEIGH FERMOR Roumeli: Travels in Northern Greece
PATRICK LEIGH FERMOR A Time of Gifts
PATRICK LEIGH FERMOR A Time to Keep Silence
D.B. WYNDHAM LEWIS AND CHARLES LEE (EDITORS) The Stuffed Owl
GEORG CHRISTOPH LICHTENBERG The Waste Books
JAKOV LIND Soul of Wood and Other Stories
H.P. LOVECRAFT AND OTHERS The Colour Out of Space
ROSE MACAULAY The Towers of Trebizond
NORMAN MAILER Miami and the Siege of Chicago
JANET MALCOLM In the Freud Archives
OSIP MANDELSTAM The Selected Poems of Osip Mandelstam
OLIVIA MANNING Fortunes of War: The Balkan Trilogy
OLIVIA MANNING School for Love
GUY DE MAUPASSANT Afloat
GUY DE MAUPASSANT Alien Hearts
JAMES MCCOURT Mawrdew Czgowchwz
HENRI MICHAUX Miserable Miracle
JESSICA MITFORD Hons and Rebels
JESSICA MITFORD Poison Penmanship
NANCY MITFORD Madame de Pompadour
HENRY DE MONTHERLANT Chaos and Night
BRIAN MOORE The Lonely Passion of Judith Hearne
ALBERTO MORAVIA Boredom
ALBERTO MORAVIA Contempt
JAN MORRIS Conundrum

ÁLVARO MUTIS The Adventures and Misadventures of Maqroll
L.H. MYERS The Root and the Flower
DARCY O'BRIEN A Way of Life, Like Any Other
YURI OLESHA Envy
IONA AND PETER OPIE The Lore and Language of Schoolchildren
IRIS OWENS After Claude
RUSSELL PAGE The Education of a Gardener
ALEXANDROS PAPADIAMANTIS The Murderess
CESARE PAVESE The Moon and the Bonfires
CESARE PAVESE The Selected Works of Cesare Pavese
LUIGI PIRANDELLO The Late Mattia Pascal
ANDREY PLATONOV The Foundation Pit
ANDREY PLATONOV Soul and Other Stories
J.F. POWERS Morte d'Urban
J.F. POWERS The Stories of J.F. Powers
CHRISTOPHER PRIEST Inverted World
RAYMOND QUENEAU We Always Treat Women Too Well
RAYMOND QUENEAU Witch Grass
JULES RENARD Nature Stories
JEAN RENOIR Renoir, My Father
GREGOR VON REZZORI Memoirs of an Anti-Semite
GREGOR VON REZZORI The Snows of Yesteryear: Portraits for an Autobiography
TIM ROBINSON Stones of Aran: Labyrinth
TIM ROBINSON Stones of Aran: Pilgrimage
FR. ROLFE Hadrian the Seventh
WILLIAM ROUGHEAD Classic Crimes
CONSTANCE ROURKE American Humor: A Study of the National Character
TAYEB SALIH Season of Migration to the North
TAYEB SALIH The Wedding of Zein
GERSHOM SCHOLEM Walter Benjamin: The Story of a Friendship
DANIEL PAUL SCHREBER Memoirs of My Nervous Illness
JAMES SCHUYLER Alfred and Guinevere
JAMES SCHUYLER What's for Dinner?
LEONARDO SCIASCIA The Day of the Owl
LEONARDO SCIASCIA Equal Danger
LEONARDO SCIASCIA The Moro Affair
LEONARDO SCIASCIA To Each His Own
LEONARDO SCIASCIA The Wine-Dark Sea
VICTOR SEGALEN René Leys
PHILIPE-PAUL DE SÉGUR Defeat: Napoleon's Russian Campaign
VICTOR SERGE The Case of Comrade Tulayev
VICTOR SERGE Unforgiving Years
SHCHEDRIN The Golovlyov Family
GEORGES SIMENON Dirty Snow
GEORGES SIMENON The Engagement
GEORGES SIMENON The Man Who Watched Trains Go By
GEORGES SIMENON Monsieur Monde Vanishes
GEORGES SIMENON Pedigree
GEORGES SIMENON The Strangers in the House
GEORGES SIMENON Three Bedrooms in Manhattan
GEORGES SIMENON Tropic Moon
GEORGES SIMENON The Widow

CHARLES SIMIC Dime-Store Alchemy: The Art of Joseph Cornell
MAY SINCLAIR Mary Olivier: A Life
TESS SLESINGER The Unpossessed: A Novel of the Thirties
VLADIMIR SOROKIN Ice
JEAN STAFFORD The Mountain Lion
CHRISTINA STEAD Letty Fox: Her Luck
GEORGE R. STEWART Names on the Land
STENDHAL The Life of Henry Brulard
ADALBERT STIFTER Rock Crystal
THEODOR STORM The Rider on the White Horse
HOWARD STURGIS Belchamber
ITALO SVEVO As a Man Grows Older
HARVEY SWADOS Nights in the Gardens of Brooklyn
A.J.A. SYMONS The Quest for Corvo
HENRY DAVID THOREAU The Journal: 1837–1861
TATYANA TOLSTAYA The Slynx
TATYANA TOLSTAYA White Walls: Collected Stories
LIONEL TRILLING The Liberal Imagination
IVAN TURGENEV Virgin Soil
JULES VALLÈS The Child
MARK VAN DOREN Shakespeare
CARL VAN VECHTEN The Tiger in the House
EDWARD LEWIS WALLANT The Tenants of Moonbloom
ROBERT WALSER Jakob von Gunten
ROBERT WALSER Selected Stories
REX WARNER Men and Gods
SYLVIA TOWNSEND WARNER Lolly Willowes
SYLVIA TOWNSEND WARNER Mr. Fortune's Maggot *and* The Salutation
SYLVIA TOWNSEND WARNER Summer Will Show
ALEKSANDER WAT My Century
C.V. WEDGWOOD The Thirty Years War
SIMONE WEIL AND RACHEL BESPALOFF War and the Iliad
GLENWAY WESCOTT Apartment in Athens
GLENWAY WESCOTT The Pilgrim Hawk
REBECCA WEST The Fountain Overflows
EDITH WHARTON The New York Stories of Edith Wharton
PATRICK WHITE Riders in the Chariot
T.H. WHITE The Goshawk
JOHN WILLIAMS Butcher's Crossing
JOHN WILLIAMS Stoner
ANGUS WILSON Anglo-Saxon Attitudes
EDMUND WILSON Memoirs of Hecate County
EDMUND WILSON To the Finland Station
RUDOLF AND MARGARET WITTKOWER Born Under Saturn
GEOFFREY WOLFF Black Sun
FRANCIS WYNDHAM The Complete Fiction
JOHN WYNDHAM The Chrysalids
STEFAN ZWEIG Beware of Pity
STEFAN ZWEIG Chess Story
STEFAN ZWEIG Journey Into the Past
STEFAN ZWEIG The Post-Office Girl